Self-Love
Crystals

CRYSTAL SPELLS AND RITUALS
FOR MAGICAL SELF-CARE

Katie Huang
Founder of ☽ LOVE BY LUNA

Illustrated by
Marie-Noël Dumont

CONTENTS

INTRODUCTION

The power of love is immense and profound. We can't see it or measure it, but there's no denying its presence. When we experience love, it's *palpable*. But love is so much more than an emotion or feeling. It's a force that can move mountains, and an energy that transcends time and space. Love permeates every aspect of our existence, shaping our thoughts, actions, and relationships. It has the capacity to nurture, inspire, and empower us, and at the core of this transformative force lies an often-neglected essence: self-love.

Practicing self-love can be challenging at times for many reasons. For starters, we live in a world that places a significant emphasis on external appearances, achievements, and material possessions. From a young age, we are bombarded with messages that suggest we need to be better, look a certain way, or accomplish specific goals to be worthy of love and acceptance. This focus on the external aspects of life not only overshadows the importance of internal worth, but also fuels a culture of constant comparison and negative self-talk that hinders our ability to love ourselves unconditionally. However, the journey of self-love is always one that is worth undertaking, because the most important relationship we can cultivate is the one we have with ourselves.

Self-love empowers us to create a life rooted in authenticity and joy by promoting radical self-acceptance. It involves recognizing our inherent worthiness, embracing our strengths and imperfections, and nurturing ourselves with compassion and kindness. When we practice self-love, we are able to honor our emotions without judgment and release ourselves from the burden of blame, shame, and guilt that often accompany past traumas or mistakes.

That said, self-love is not a destination but an ongoing journey—one that requires patience, honesty, and an unwavering commitment to oneself. Just as a seed takes time to grow into a mighty tree, self-love is an ever-evolving process that gradually unfolds. It calls us to show up for ourselves every day with courage and tenderness, and asks us to challenge the patterns and beliefs that hold us back.

If you're ready to let go of fear and open your heart to the most potent source of healing, this book will guide you every step of the way as you embark on your self-love journey. Throughout its pages, you'll explore the benefits of crystal healing and how it can be used to transform your relationship to love, along with spells, rituals, and meditations to cultivate compassion and harmony within. As you move forward, remember: each day presents an opportunity to embrace who you are, and when you do, you can unlock your true potential.

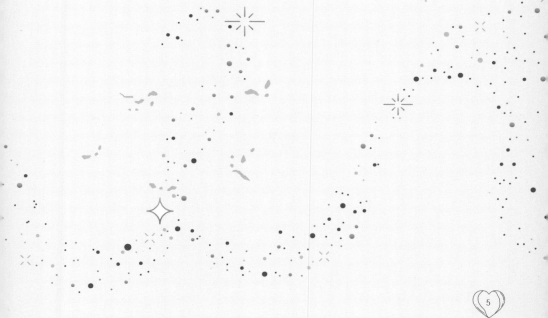

HOW TO USE THIS BOOK

Welcome to the nourishing realm of *Self-Love Crystals.* This book is your comprehensive guide to harnessing the transformative power of crystals for cultivating self-love and personal growth. To make the most of your journey, here's tips on how to use this book, and a few things to know before you read.

- Start with Crystal Healing 101: This section covers all the basics, providing you with a solid foundation in crystal healing. Explore topics such as how crystal healing works, crystal selection, charging and cleansing methods, and an introduction to the chakras.

- Dive into Self-Love Crystals: In the second part of the book, we'll explore thirty powerful crystals for self-love. Each crystal is accompanied by its individual properties, uses, and suggested practices. Familiarize yourself with these crystals, their unique energies, and how they can support you on you on your self-love journey.

- Explore Spells, Rituals, and Meditations: The third section of the book is dedicated to empowering you with a variety of crystal healing practices. Here, you will find spells, rituals, and meditations designed to support different aspects of self-love. Feel free to explore these practices in any order that resonates with you.

THINGS TO KNOW BEFORE YOU READ

- Your intention is the star of the show. While the crystals and practices that we explore are amazing tools, it's your intention that infuses them with power. So, set clear intentions and let them guide your exploration of self-love.

- Personalize your practice. I encourage you to tailor the practices in this book to your unique preferences and needs. Feel free to modify the ingredients in any of the spells and rituals to your liking. If a crystal or practice doesn't resonate with you, omit it or swap it out for one that does.

- When substituting an ingredient, replace it with one that has similar energetic properties for best results. For instance, if a spell calls for rose quartz, use another pink crystal or love-related stone in its place, such as rhodonite or morganite. Clear quartz can also be used in place of any crystal.

- The spells and rituals in this book do not call for specific crystal shapes to be used. You can research which shapes or sizes may work best for you, or use the shapes recommended in the artwork.

- When in doubt, follow your intuition. If you're unsure of what crystal to work with, trust your gut. Your intuition knows what you need, so don't be afraid to lean into your inner knowing.

DISCLAIMER

The information provided in this book does not claim to diagnose, treat, cure, or prevent any illness, and should not be used as a substitute for conventional medicine or psychological treatment. Always consult a healthcare professional before using any holistic therapies such as crystal healing or herbal medicine, particularly if you have a known medical condition or if you are pregnant or nursing. There is the possibility of allergic or other adverse reactions from the use of any ingredients, essential oils, or other items mentioned in this book. By using this book you acknowledge and accept all risks and responsibilities concerning your actions as a result of using any information provided herein.

Have you ever been drawn to the beauty and energy of crystals? Maybe you have memories of collecting them as a child or have recently caught yourself eyeing one in a store window. Or perhaps you've heard about crystal healing from a friend and are curious to learn more. No matter the case, you're in the right place.

Crystal healing is an ancient practice that has been used for centuries to promote physical, emotional, and spiritual wellbeing. In this section, we'll cover how crystal healing works, crystal selection, cleansing and charging tips, as well as an introduction to chakras. Let's begin!

CRYSTAL
HEALING
101

HOW CRYSTAL HEALING WORKS

Among the many gifts that Mother Earth provides us, crystals are one of its greatest treasures. There are over four thousand different types of minerals that we currently know of, which come in a dazzling array of colors, shapes, and sizes. Humans have long been fascinated by these captivating gems and their potential healing abilities. One of the first historical references to the use of crystals comes from the ancient Sumerians, who included them in their magickal healing formulas and inlays of their finest artwork around 4000 BCE. Similarly, Ancient Egyptians used lapis lazuli and carnelian in their jewelry, wearing them as talismans for protection. Healing crystals such as jade and turquoise were also central to Chinese medicine for almost five thousand years, and continue to be used to this day.

It's clear that humans have shared a special connection with crystals throughout the ages, and that sentiment still rings true now. Crystal healing continues to be a popular and effective practice for promoting overall wellbeing and mindfulness. But the ways in which crystals are used for healing are just as diverse as the crystals themselves. From sleep spells to abundance rituals, there are countless ways to incorporate crystals into your day-to-day life, but how you choose to work with them is ultimately up to you. While crystals are believed to carry unique energetic properties and benefits, they

aren't capable of working miracles on their own. Rather, their true magick resides within the person who uses them—*you*.

Like any other tool for mindfulness, crystals are here to help you tap in to your inner power. Think of them like your very own personal coaching team—they won't do the work for you, but they will act as facilitators and catalysts for your growth. In essence, crystals can position you for success by giving you a gentle nudge when your mind starts to slip toward negative thoughts, or an extra push when you need to break through limiting patterns. When you hold or wear a crystal, you are essentially inviting its energy into your field, aligning yourself with its unique frequency and properties. In this sense, crystals can serve as tangible reminders of the intentions you've set, or a mindset you wish to adopt.

CRYSTAL SELECTION

With so many options available, choosing which crystals to work with can feel like a daunting task, but don't fret! The good news is, you don't have to research every crystal's properties in order to make the "right" choice, because the truth is that there is no better guide than your own intuition. While certain stones are associated with specific energies, every crystal is unique, and may contain different messages for different people. So if you pick up a special vibe or insight from a stone, don't be afraid to lean into it. Trusting your gut is key when selecting the crystals that will work best for you. After all, you know your own needs and desires better than anyone else. Follow your instincts, and you can't go wrong.

However, if you're still having trouble deciding, there are a few guidelines that can help you sift through your options. Choosing a stone based on its color is an easy place to start. Are you drawn to fiery hues that energize your spirit or calming, cooler tones that invoke a sense of inner peace? Pick a color to match your mood.

If you're more of a tactile person, you might base your decision on how a crystal physically feels. Hold it in your hand and rub it against your fingers. Does it feel waxy, smooth, or bumpy? Notice what textures stimulate you. Keep in mind that many crystals come in tumbled (polished) and rough (raw) varieties.

A crystal's shape is another factor to consider, as it can affect the way that energy is sent and received. For instance, a cube's sturdy structure makes it ideal for grounding practices, while a sphere emits energy evenly in all directions. Additionally, pyramids can be used for manifestation, or points and towers for amplifying intentions.

Lastly, if you have a particular intention or energy in mind, choosing a stone based on its properties is a good option. You might search for stones for love, abundance, protection, clarity, motivation, intuition, creativity, grounding, focus, or stress-relief. These are just a few examples but should give you a helpful starting point.

CRYSTAL CARE

Crystals are amazing tools for energy work, but like many tools, they require care and maintenance to function at their best. This means cleansing and charging your crystals regularly to ensure that they are always vibrating at their highest frequency. While this applies to most gems, there are a few exceptions to the rule, like selenite, which is considered a self-cleansing stone.

Cleansing crystals involves removing negative energy or unwanted frequencies that may have accumulated over time, returning the stone to its natural, clean state. On the other hand, charging crystals involves adding energy to the stone, replenishing its energy if it has been depleted. How often you should cleanse and charge your crystals depends on how frequently you use them. Generally speaking, it is recommended that you cleanse and charge your crystals once a month, but you can adjust this schedule based on your intuition and the specific needs of your crystals.

It's worth noting that not all cleansing and charging methods are safe for every type of crystal, so it's important to research the specific stone you are working with and make sure the method you choose is appropriate for it.

TOOLS TO CLEANSE CRYSTALS WITH

Water

Water is one of the most traditional and widely used cleansing methods for purifying stones. Soaking a stone in water helps to remove any physical energetic residue or impurities that may be clinging to its surface. To cleanse yours, place your crystal in a bowl of purified water overnight and give it an extra rinse when you're done. *Please note that some stones may dissolve or become damaged when they come in contact with water. As a general rule of thumb, most stones ending in "-ite" are not water safe, such as selenite, calcite, hematite, pyrite, fluorite, malachite, labradorite, etc.*

Smoke

Using smoke to cleanse crystals is a gentle and safe method that can be used on any stone. It involves lighting incense or dried herbs and holding the stone in its smoke for a few minutes until you feel it is cleansed. We recommend performing this outside or cracking a window when indoors to ensure proper ventilation. There are many types of incense and herbs you can use, but frankincense, cedar, rosemary, and garden sage are favored for their purification properties. Perhaps the best benefit of smoke cleansing is that there is no risk of damaging your stone.

Sound

Sound cleansing uses sound waves to break up stagnant or negative energy that may be attached to a crystal. When a sound is created, it moves through the air as a series of vibrations. These vibrations can permeate stones and cause them to vibrate at a certain frequency, creating a harmonic balance that releases negativity. Sound healing can be performed with a singing bowl, tuning fork, chimes, or any musical instrument. Place your crystal near the source of sound, allowing it to bathe in its vibrations for a few minutes. Due to its non-invasive and gentle nature, sound cleansing is safe for all stones, and won't alter or damage the surface of a crystal.

Salt

Salt has been used as a cleansing method for centuries, as many ancient cultures believed in its ability to absorb toxins and negativity. To use this method, gather a glass or ceramic bowl that is large enough to hold your crystal, along with salt. You can use sea salt or pink Himalayan salt. Pour enough salt into the container to form a layer at the bottom that's at least one to two inches deep (or more if you're working with a larger stone). Bury your crystal in the center of the bowl, making sure it is completely covered by salt. Let it sit for a few hours, or overnight if possible. Afterward, remove the crystal and gently wipe it with a cloth to remove any remaining salt. *Please note that certain stones are sensitive to salt and should not be used with this method, such as turquoise, malachite, calcite, amber, moonstone, opal, selenite, carnelian, bloodstone, topaz, and azurite.*

Sunlight

Sunlight is can be used to cleanse your crystals and also to charge them. I suggest setting your stones outside in daylight (or on a windowsill if you prefer) for six to twelve hours for best results. However, if you're short on time, even a thirty minute soak in the sun's rays will do. This method is still effective even when it's overcast, as the sun's powerful energy can be received through the clouds. That said, some crystals like aventurine, amethyst, citrine, and rose quartz are prone to fading when exposed to sunlight for extended periods, so be careful of where you choose to place them.

Moonlight

Like sunlight, moonlight can also be used for both cleansing and charging. When crystals are exposed to moonlight, the energy of the moon is absorbed by the crystals, which can cleanse them of negative energy or restore them to their full power. To use this method, simply place your stones outside or near a window where they can be exposed to moonlight. It's best to leave them out overnight but even a few hours can be beneficial. While you can perform this under any lunar phase, the energy of the new moon is particularly aligned with cleansing, while the full moon is suited to charging.

Crystals

Some crystals have the power to purify and recharge the energy of other stones. For instance, selenite and blue kyanite can be used for cleansing, citrine for charging, and clear quartz or amethyst for both charging and cleansing. Simply place your desired stone on top of or near these crystals for a few hours.

Visualization

Visualization is a cleansing technique that harnesses the power of your thoughts. To cleanse a stone, imagine a bright white light surrounding the crystal, penetrating it, and clearing away any negative energy or impurities. You can also visualize yourself pouring your own positive energy into the stone, infusing it with renewed vitality and purpose. The key is to focus your mind on the intention of clearing the crystal and picturing exactly what you desire—a pure, fresh stone bathed in positive vibrations. This method can be used with any stone.

CHAKRAS

If you're new to energy work, there's a good chance you've heard the word chakra before. But what exactly is a chakra, and how does it relate to crystal healing? Simply put, chakras are energy centers located throughout the body that are thought to play a vital role in physical, emotional, and spiritual wellbeing. There are seven main chakras that run from the base of the spine to the top of the head, each corresponding to a specific area of the body and emotional state.

When our chakras are balanced and open, energy is believed to flow freely and smoothly throughout the body, fostering a sense of harmony within oneself. However, if a chakra becomes blocked or unbalanced, this can lead to physical or emotional discomfort. A blocked chakra is typically a sign that something isn't working on an internal level, which can manifest in a variety of ways. For instance, someone with a blocked throat chakra may experience difficulty communicating or expressing themselves.

An easy way to bring our chakras back into alignment is through crystal healing. Crystals have unique energetic properties that can affect the energy flow within the chakras. Each stone has a specific vibrational frequency that corresponds to one or more of the seven chakras. When a crystal is placed on or near a chakra, its energy resonates with the frequency of the chakra, helping to remove blockages, negativity, and restore balance.

Many of the spells, rituals, and meditations in this book refer to chakras, so use the following descriptions as a reference when navigating your self-love practices. While most love-related issues deal with the heart chakra, don't ignore the others! A lack of energy or excess energy in any of the chakras can impact your relationship with love, whether by affecting your sense of security, confidence, and more.

ROOT CHAKRA

Location:
Base of the spine

Associated color:
Red

Favorite root chakra stones:
Red jasper, garnet, bloodstone, hematite, obsidian, black tourmaline

As the first chakra, the root chakra (also known as the base chakra) represents our foundation and connection to the earth. It governs our basic needs for survival such as shelter, food, and safety. A balanced root chakra leads to feelings of stability and security while an unbalanced one can cause fear, anxiety, and a lack of trust in oneself and others. Those with a blocked root chakra may feel like they can't find their footing in the world. They may struggle with staying grounded and have difficulty setting and maintaining healthy boundaries.

SACRAL CHAKRA

Location:
Lower abdomen below the navel

Associated color:
Orange

Favorite sacral chakra stones:
Carnelian, moonstone, tangerine quartz, orange calcite, aragonite, sunstone

The second chakra is the sacral chakra. It is associated with our emotional body and sensuality, and controls our ability to experience pleasure, creativity, and joy. This chakra is connected to the element of water, which symbolizes the adaptability and fluidity of our ever-changing emotions. When this chakra is balanced, we are able to enjoy the simple pleasures of life and experience intimacy and connection with others. We feel creative and comfortable with our sexuality and can express our desires without fear. When this chakra is unbalanced, we may repress our emotions due to fear or shame. We may also struggle with addiction, a lack of creativity, or have difficulty forming healthy relationships.

SOLAR PLEXUS CHAKRA

Location:
Upper abdomen

Associated color:
Yellow

Favorite solar plexus chakra stones:
Citrine, pyrite, gold tiger's eye, honey calcite, amber, lemon quartz

The third chakra, the solar plexus chakra, represents our personal power, confidence, and self-esteem. A balanced solar plexus chakra produces a strong sense of self-worth and self-assurance that helps us take action toward our goals. When this chakra is unbalanced or underactive, we may struggle with low self-esteem and confidence. We may feel powerless over a situation and have difficulty asserting ourselves or making decisions. On the other hand, an overactive solar plexus chakra may cause us to become domineering or manipulative in our interactions with others. It may also result in excessively competitive, controlling, or aggressive behaviors.

HEART CHAKRA

Location:
Center of chest

Associated color:
Green or pink

Favorite heart chakra stones:
Green aventurine, jade, malachite, moss agate, rose quartz, rhodonite, morganite

As the fourth chakra, the heart chakra serves as a bridge between the lower and upper chakras, balancing the material and spiritual worlds. It governs our ability to love and connect with others, as well as ourselves. When this chakra is balanced, we are able to experience unconditional love in its purest form and a deep sense of empathy toward others. Our heart remains open, allowing us to give and receive love with ease. However, when this chakra becomes unbalanced, it can lead to feelings of loneliness and isolation. We may be possessive or jealous in our relationships or struggle with codependency.

THROAT CHAKRA

Location:
Center of the neck

Associated color:
Blue

Favorite throat chakra stones:
Blue sodalite, chrysocolla, aquamarine, blue calcite, celestite, amazonite, blue lace agate

The fifth chakra, or throat chakra, is associated with communication. It affects our ability to speak truthfully and express our thoughts and emotions effectively. A balanced throat chakra promotes healthy self-expression that allows us to communicate with others in an honest and authentic way. Those with a blocked throat chakra may exhibit a fear of speaking or excessive shyness. They may struggle to find the right words to say, causing them to feel unheard or misunderstood.

THIRD EYE CHAKRA

Location:
Center of forehead, between the eyebrows

Associated color:
Indigo or purple

Favorite third eye chakra stones:
Amethyst, lapis lazuli, labradorite, lepidolite, iolite, fluorite, azurite

The sixth chakra is the third eye chakra. Also called the brow chakra, it speaks to our intuition, perception, imagination, and spiritual awareness. When in balance, this chakra supports us in trusting our gut and listening to our inner wisdom. It allows us to see the "bigger" picture and reveals insights from our dreams. In contrast, an unbalanced third eye chakra can lead to confusion, a lack of direction, and a feeling of being lost. We may struggle to make decisions and find it challenging to connect with our inner self.

CROWN CHAKRA

Location:
Top of the head

Associated color:
Violet or white

Favorite crown chakra stones:
Clear quartz, selenite, white howlite, sugilite, herkimer diamond, rainbow moonstone

The final, seventh chakra is called the crown chakra. It represents our connection to the universe and spiritual consciousness. A balanced crown chakra can lead to a deeper sense of purpose and peace that helps us rise above earthly problems. When out of balance, we may feel cut off from our spirituality, choosing to focus on materialistic pursuits. This may also lead to cynicism, apathy, or a lack of inspiration or faith. A person with a blocked crown chakra may get stuck in their way of thinking and exhibit an unwillingness to be open to other ideas or knowledge.

Each crystal in the vast world of gemstones is truly unique, possessing its own distinct energy and characteristics. Just as each person is one-of-a-kind, crystals hold their own special vibrations and properties that make them valuable allies on our self-love journey. While some crystals may be more directly associated with love and compassion, it's important to remember that self-love has many dimensions. It's not just about opening our hearts to kindness, but developing self-awareness of the patterns and behaviors that are no longer serving us. That said, the crystals in this chapter all support self-love in different ways, teaching valuable lessons in honoring emotions, harnessing confidence, stimulating forgiveness, setting boundaries, and more. Ultimately, any crystal can be used to cultivate a connection with your inner self, so know that this list isn't exhaustive. As always, I encourage you to explore the diverse world of crystals and discover the ones that speak to your heart. It is also important to remember that crystals are not magickal cure-alls, but rather tools that can support and amplify your own efforts and intentions.

SELF-LOVE CRYSTALS

ROSE QUARTZ

There's a reason why rose quartz is known as the premier stone of love and compassion. According to ancient lore, Cupid, the Roman god of desire, and Eros, the Greek god of love, presented it as a gift to the earth to spread love and passion among people. Favored for its gorgeous, delicate pink hue, rose quartz continues to inspire us today by teaching us how to lead with love and find beauty in the world around us. Radiating with gentle, soothing energy, this comforting crystal is the perfect companion to have by your side when tending to matters of the heart. Sensitive, yet supportive, it assists in healing the emotional body and encouraging forgiveness and self-acceptance. Sometimes it's difficult to treat ourselves with the same level of kindness and empathy that we show toward others, but this crystal serves as an important reminder that we are always worthy of love. By working with rose quartz, we can release negative self-talk and judgments that keep us stuck in limiting patterns, and learn to love and accept ourselves for who we are.

Chakra:
Heart

Affirmation:
I am worthy of love and I choose to love and accept myself fully and completely.

Ritual: Leave the stress of the day behind and ease into a peaceful environment by keeping rose quartz at the stopping point of your home. The stopping point is wherever you pause to take off your shoes, put down your keys, or remove your purse or backpack. This could be an entryway table, mudroom bench, kitchen counter, or any other area. Placing this crystal here acts like an energetic air purifier, filtering your aura of negativity and replacing it with currents of love. If you feel particularly frazzled after a long day, take an extra moment at your stopping point and hold this stone to your heart for one minute for instant relaxation.

AMETHYST

Kick bad habits to the curb with amethyst. This crystal has long been associated with spiritual growth and self-awareness. It gets its name from the Greek word *"amethystos"* meaning "not drunken," and today continues to be known as the fabled "sobriety stone" due to its ability to promote clarity of thought. Its high vibrational energy stimulates the third eye and crown chakras, helping us connect with our intuition and higher selves. By working with amethyst, we are able to reach a place of quiet contemplation that allows our inner voice to be heard. What is the best decision we can make for ourselves in this moment? What actions serve our greatest good? Meditating with amethyst creates space for these questions to be asked and provides opportunities to break free from the toxic cycles and compulsions that keep us trapped in lower vibrations.

If you've found yourself slipping into negative patterns or indulging in vices that prevent you from truly loving yourself, amethyst can help you cut those ties. Reach for it whenever you need to resist temptation and you'll instantly feel supported by its purifying aura. By forming a barrier around our energy field, amethyst prevents unwanted energies from entering and disrupting our inner peace. Its calming energy helps to soothe our emotions and clear our minds, allowing us to see things from a more positive perspective.

Chakra:
Third eye, crown

Affirmation:
I trust my intuition and listen to my inner voice. My mind is clear and focused. I am free of negative influences.

Ritual: For a good night's sleep, meditate with amethyst before bed. Hold your crystal as you allow its calming frequency to slowly release tension and stress from your mind. Once you've come to a quiet place, set an intention for peaceful dreams such as, "Calming thoughts will fill my dreams. I am ready to rest." Place the crystal on your nightstand or beneath your pillow to promote deep sleep.

MORGANITE

Finding the strength to love oneself can be a difficult journey, especially where trauma or heartbreak is concerned, but morganite teaches us that true love starts from within. Don't be fooled by its delicate, soft pink hues; this gem is one of the strongest heart healers in the crystal kingdom. A stone of strong emotions, it works its magick by stirring up any hidden feelings we may secretly be harboring, like anger or resentment, and giving us the courage and confidence to address them. By allowing these emotions to rise to the surface, morganite helps us clear out any negativity surrounding our heart and puts us on the path to healing old emotional wounds.

If the thought of digging into your vulnerabilities sounds intimidating, don't worry—morganite won't force you into anything you're not ready for. This crystal has a light and serene energy that provides a safe space for you to open your heart to self-love. If you tend to look outside of yourself for validation or affection, use this stone to turn your attention inward and remind you of your heart's power. Morganite is also perfect for anyone who has difficulty opening up emotionally or expressing themselves. This crystal can guide you through the process of loving yourself, even if it feels like the world is against you. It encourages you to be kind and compassionate to yourself, which is often the first step in healing from any emotional pain.

Chakra:
Heart

Affirmation:
I am strong and resilient. I am open to giving and receiving love unconditionally. I trust in the power of my heart to guide me.

Ritual: Open your heart to healing by meditating with morganite. Hold the stone over your chest and connect to its nurturing energy. Visualize a small ball of pink light emanating from the center of the stone, growing bigger and brighter with every breath you take. When the light is roughly the size of a basketball, focus on directing it into your heart, filling it up to the brim with love until it is fully absorbed.

CARNELIAN

Carnelian is a vibrant and captivating crystal. Its bold orange color is reminiscent of a warm, comforting fire, and its energy is just as stimulating. This stone connects us to our passions and gives us the courage to go after our deepest desires. If you've found that your days have grown dull or you feel disconnected from the world, use carnelian to reignite your zest for life and fan the flames of your desires. It's time to follow your bliss! Motivating and inspiring, this stone breathes new life into everything it touches. It is also believed to be one of the best crystals for working through sexual blockages, as its connection to the sacral chakra addresses libido.

Carnelian is a powerful tool for self-love, as it promotes inner child healing, helping us tap into our carefree, playful side. This can be especially beneficial for those who have experienced emotional trauma or have had to grow up too quickly. When we connect with carnelian, we are encouraged to embrace creativity, spontaneity, and joy, as well as our sensuality. It reminds us that it's okay to let loose and have fun, and that we don't always have to take life so seriously. Carnelian is also known to support self-expression, giving us the freedom to be our most authentic selves. It allows us to communicate our emotional needs without fear, shame, or guilt, and find pleasure in life's juiciest moments.

Chakra:
Root, sacral, heart

Affirmation:
I embrace my inner child. I am whole and complete, and I love and accept myself unconditionally.

Ritual: Meditate with this stone to rev up your inner fire. Hold it in your hand and envision a spark igniting in your sacral chakra (in the lower abdomen, below the navel). Feel the vibrant energy of carnelian filling your body with confidence and motivation, growing the spark into a strong flame. Imagine it burning brightly as it spreads warmth and vitality through your entire body, making you feel alive.

RHODONITE

Rhodonite can help you forgive even the deepest hurts. This stone of compassion excels in healing emotional scars and cultivating feelings of self-worth. While its gorgeous pink color nourishes and opens the heart, its darker patches resonate with the root chakra, speaking to our sense of safety and security. If past experiences or relationships have left you feeling jaded, bitter, or riddled with mistrust, rhodonite can be a supportive ally in deconstructing the emotional barriers that are preventing you from moving forward.

The first step in forgiving someone means letting go of the hurt or anger we feel toward them—but this is easier said than done. In order to release that pain, we have to tear down those walls. It can be scary to let go of something that has become so familiar, especially when we feel vulnerable, but this is where rhodonite thrives. This crystal stimulates forgiveness and self-acceptance by encouraging a heart-centered perspective, making it easier for us to tap into our own feelings of compassion and empathy, even toward people who have hurt us. It promotes mutual understanding and acceptance in relationships, allowing us to see both sides of an issue while still maintaining our own point of view. When we work with this stone, we are being asked to let go of negative emotions and unhealthy attitudes so that we can embrace compromise from a place of trust and authenticity.

Chakra:
Root, heart

Affirmation:
I release any negative emotions and open my heart to self-love and acceptance.

Ritual: Ease tension by using rhodonite in a breath work ritual. Come to a seated position and hold the crystal in your hands. Allow its compassionate energy to wash over your heart, dislodging any bitter feelings as they rise to the surface. On the inhale, imagine breathing in love and positivity. On the exhale, focus on breathing out negativity and resentment. Repeat this for ten to twenty breath cycles.

MALACHITE

Malachite is a powerful crystal that has been used for centuries to promote inner transformation, and it's not hard to see why. A potent heart-opening stone, its swirling green shades embody the healing power of nature, acting as a catalyst for personal growth. Malachite is an excellent crystal for those who are serious about making profound, positive changes in their life, especially in regards to love. Whereas rose quartz provides a gentle energy and nurturing touch, malachite takes on a more "tough love" approach. Think of it as that one person you can always count on for honest, unfiltered advice.

This crystal acts as a warning signal for anything that isn't in alignment with our highest good. It shines a light on the patterns that are holding us back, and helps us face the truth about our relationships, allowing us to see what is working and what is not. This can be a difficult process, as it often involves confronting uncomfortable truths about ourselves and our partners. However, with this stone by our side, we can feel empowered to take action and uncover the root of our issues. If you're ready to turn over a new leaf, use this stone to gain the courage to step out of your comfort zone and truly break through barriers to love.

Chakra:
Heart

Affirmation:
I release old patterns and beliefs that no longer serve me, making new room for growth and positive changes in my life.

Ritual: Use malachite to cleanse and purify your energy. Hold it in your hand and imagine any negative or stagnant energy being absorbed by the stone. Visualize the rich, green color of malachite clearing away any blockages and revitalizing your energy field. Then pass the stone over your body in sweeping motions from head to toe, visualizing it carrying away unwanted attachments.

RHODOCHROSITE

At first glance, it's easy to confuse rhodochrosite with rhodonite, but besides their similar names and color, they're quite different in terms of energy. Whereas rhodonite focuses more on forgiveness, joy is the name of the game where rhodochrosite is concerned. This is a wonderful crystal to work with when you need to brighten your outlook on love and reclaim your sense of wonder. A cheerful and radiant stone, rhodochrosite uplifts the spirit and promotes a sunny disposition. By infusing the heart center with positive vibrations, it gives us the courage to be vulnerable as well as the confidence to love again.

This little pink gemstone is your friend when it comes to boosting self-esteem (especially when recovering from a breakup), as it directs love toward the self, first and foremost. If you tend to prioritize others' needs above your own, this is a great stone to shift the focus back to you. Not only will it help you develop a deeper appreciation for who you are, it also supports you in recognizing your unique gifts and infinite potential. With rhodochrosite by your side, you'll be able to shrug off your inner critic and bathe yourself in waves of compassion that allow your heart to expand and experience love at its fullest.

Chakra:
Heart

Affirmation:
I radiate positivity and compassion toward myself and others, knowing that I am worthy and deserving of all the good that comes my way.

Ritual: Hold your crystal in your hand and take a few deep breaths. Visualize a bright pink light emanating from the stone, filling your body with warmth and positivity. Repeat the affirmation, "I am worthy of love and respect," aloud three times. Hold the stone to your heart and visualize the pink light spreading outward, enveloping your entire being in a nourishing embrace. Continue soaking in this current of divine love for a few minutes, then gently open your eyes.

MOONSTONE

Moonstone represents a fresh start. This enchanting crystal is perfect for turning over a new leaf, as its fertile energies stimulate growth and provide a rich foundation for intentions to flourish. While the energy of some stones can feel jarring or intense (especially those related to transformation), moonstone is incredibly gentle, making it an excellent choice for sensitive individuals. It enhances adaptability and flexibility, enabling us to be more open to new experiences and ideas. This openness allows for shifts in perspectives and behaviors that support personal growth.

As its name suggests, moonstone has a strong connection to the moon and the divine feminine—speaking to our emotions and intuition. Like the moon, this stone reminds us of our cyclical nature and our ability to change, grow, and evolve as we move through different phases of life. Working with moonstone calls us to access our inner wisdom by exploring the thoughts, feelings, desires, and messages that often go unnoticed in our busy lives. By calming the mind and balancing our emotions, moonstone creates a receptive space for intuitive insights to arise. That said, this crystal is also highly suited for dreamwork, as it helps us tap in to higher states of consciousness and integrate dream insights into our waking lives.

Chakra:
Sacral, solar plexus, third eye

Affirmation:
I embrace the magick of new beginnings, and the wisdom of my heart. My sensitivity is my superpower.

Ritual: Use moonstone to enhance dream recall. Keep a piece of moonstone by your bedside or under your pillow to encourage vivid and insightful dreams. Upon waking, take a moment to reflect on the symbols, emotions, or messages that emerged during your dream. Explore what they mean to you personally and suspend the need to "make sense" of everything. If you start to feel confused or frustrated, hold moonstone in your hand to connect to your intuitive wisdom.

UNAKITE

If you want to build a lasting relationship with self-love, unakite is the crystal you need. Just like a beautiful garden, our seeds of self-love need nurturing, attention, and the right conditions to flourish, and unakite is here to support us along our journey. Associated with the earth, this crystal serves as a steady source of renewing, healing, and grounding energies, making it an ideal companion for spiritual rebirth. It reminds us that growth cannot be rushed or achieved through shortcuts but requires consistent effort and dedication. The beauty of unakite is that it allows our healing and evolution to unfold at our own unique pace. This is a very patient and stable energy that is well suited toward setting and achieving small, daily goals.

Unakite is also a stone of vision. It stimulates the third eye and heart chakras, enhancing intuition, insight, and spiritual awareness. Working with this stone enables us to gain clarity on our goals and make decisions from a place of authenticity. At the start of any new cycle, doubts inevitably arise. Are we truly ready for change? What happens if we fail? Is the path we're taking the "right" one? In these instances, unakite teaches us to trust our gut, and that it's never too late to start following our dreams. By instilling perseverance and resilience, this stone allows us to overcome emotional obstacles and reminds us that setbacks and challenges are a natural part of life.

Chakra:
Heart, third eye

Affirmation:
I navigate the process of healing and awakening with love and gratitude.

Ritual: Tune in to the present moment with unakite. Hold the crystal in your hands and begin to count down from the number ten in your mind, focusing on your breath. Make each inhale and exhale longer and slower than the one before it. Once you've finished, sit for a few minutes in silence, allowing yourself to just be. If your mind starts to wander, rub your crystal in your hands to shift your attention back to the present and repeat the countdown process again.

PERIDOT

Peridot is a stunning crystal with a bright and refreshing energy. Working with this stone feels like catching a glimmer of sunshine through the trees that instantly carries your worries away. While the color green is often associated with envy, nothing could be further from the truth where this stone is concerned. Working like a deep cleanser for the soul, peridot washes away any salty sentiments that are preventing us from living our best life. Oftentimes, we cling onto jealousy, bitterness, and hatred without even knowing it, but this only keeps us from experiencing the unconditional love that we deserve.

Where peridot works its magick is by loosening the grip that these negative emotions have on our heart and replacing them with optimism and joy. It also tunes us in to all the positive qualities that we have to offer. By boosting our confidence and self-esteem, this stone cultivates an abundance mindset that helps us realize our one-of-a-kind sparkle and true worth. If you feel like you've lost your mojo or that special pep in your step, use this stone to revitalize your spirit and kick your self-love practices into a higher gear. Treat yourself to a relaxing massage, buy your favorite dessert, or book that trip you've always wanted to take. It's okay to spoil yourself every once in a while.

Chakra:
Heart

Affirmation:
I choose love and joy each day. I am a magnet for abundance and prosperity.

Ritual: Brighten your mood with peridot. Hold the crystal in your hand and align with its joyful energy. Close your eyes and think about a few of your favorite things. This could be a happy memory, your pet's face, or a favorite song or meal. Focus on whatever you choose in your mind and the feeling it creates. Now expand that feeling until it washes over your entire body, bathing you in positivity.

BLACK TOURMALINE

Learning how to protect our heart is a crucial part of self-love. A premier stone of protection, black tourmaline serves as a shield against negativity—blocking and removing unwanted energy from the home, mind, body, and spirit. When we go through rough or draining times, we often don't realize the negativity building up within us and our surroundings. Left unattended, this energy can start to accumulate and clog up our heart space, but black tourmaline helps us release it. Meditating with this stone for even just a few minutes can help to unwind any stress and melt away bad moods.

Black tourmaline also assists with boundary setting. This is especially useful for those who work in highly stressful environments, deal with toxic people or situations, or have a tendency to take on the emotions of others. If someone is bothering you and physically separating yourself from them isn't an option, use this stone to enforce healthy boundaries and guard your energy so you don't end up drained. Its connection to the root chakra, which governs our sense of security, grounds and keeps us rooted in the present moment. No matter what is happening around us, this crystal helps us remain calm and levelheaded through the chaos.

Chakra:
Root

Affirmation:
I am protected and surrounded by a shield of positive energy, allowing only love and light to enter my space.

Ritual: Create a protective shield around your home by placing a piece of black tourmaline by your front door. Before you set it down, use the crystal to trace the outline of the door, forming an energetic seal against outside influences, then speak the following affirmation aloud: "I banish negativity from entering this space. I am safe at all times."

KUNZITE

If you've kept your heart guarded for far too long, kunzite is the crystal you need. This stone is not only a powerful healer of the emotional body, but also a catalyst for spiritual growth and connection. Its soothing vibrations promote tranquility and inner peace, offering a source of solace during challenging times. At the core of this crystal's healing properties is its capacity to dissolve stagnant energy and emotional blockages. It assists in breaking down walls and barriers erected as a result of past emotional pain, allowing us to experience the transformative power of forgiveness and compassion. By helping us release resentments and grudges, this stone makes room for healing and paves the way for new, positive experiences to enter our lives.

Dubbed the stone of emotion, kunzite opens and connects the heart to the mind, creating a harmonious balance between the two. By helping us explore our feelings with openness and honesty, this stone allows us to gain a deeper understanding of ourselves and the emotional patterns that are holding us back. Kunzite also teaches us the art of self-love and self-acceptance. This crystal reminds us of our inherent worthiness and guides us to embrace all aspects of ourselves—even the vulnerable and tender parts.

Chakra:
Throat, heart, third eye, crown

Affirmation:
I release past pain and present anxieties. I am filled with a vibration of divine love.

Ritual: Use kunzite in a gratitude ritual. Create a small altar with kunzite as the centerpiece. Surround the crystal with items that represent gratitude, such as dried flowers (lillies, carnations, tulips, and roses in particular), a gratitude journal or a list of things you're grateful for, or photographs of loved ones. Take a moment to reflect on the positive forces in your life and express your appreciation for each of them. Hold the kunzite in your hand and infuse it with your feelings of joy and gratitude, then place it somewhere visible. It will serve as a daily reminder of the abundance of love and blessings that surround you.

GREEN AVENTURINE

Known as the stone of opportunity, and considered to be one of the luckiest crystals, green aventurine is a beacon of good fortune. Its lush, invigorating hue symbolizes new beginnings, fertility, and growth, and its energy paves the way for a fresh start. This stone encourages you to leave limiting beliefs, old patterns, and outdated habits behind so that you can make room to receive abundance in your life, both materially and spiritually. Not only can this crystal bring new opportunities to your door, but it nurtures your sense of self-worth, helping you cultivate abundance within.

When you work with this crystal, take some time to reflect on your beliefs about money, success, and resources. Notice if you have a tendency to focus on lack and scarcity or if you have a positive outlook on life. If you tend to lean toward the former, use green aventurine to tap into the beauty, prosperity, and love that surrounds you. Shift away from a scarcity mindset to one of abundance is by practicing gratitude. Each morning, focus on the things in your life that you're grateful for. This could be as simple as having a roof over your head or clean air to breathe. Affirm that abundance is available to you and that you are worthy of receiving it.

Chakra:
Heart

Affirmation:
I allow love and positivity to flow freely within me and radiate outward, attracting joy and abundance into my life.

Ritual: Use green aventurine to connect to the element of earth. Find a serene outdoor setting, such as a park or garden, and bring this crystal with you. Sit or stand in a comfortable position, close your eyes, and hold your stone in your hand. Take deep breaths, feeling the earth beneath your feet and the gentle breeze on your skin. Tune in to the harmonizing essence of the stone and visualize yourself merging with the surrounding nature and becoming one.

PINK CALCITE

Pink calcite, also known as mangano calcite, is a stone of inner peace and healing. Its soothing and stabilizing presence feels like slipping under your favorite weighted blanket, creating a safe and secure space to work through your emotions, no matter how heavy or challenging they may be. If you're dealing with trauma or raw grief, this crystal can help you regain your emotional balance one step at a time, free from pressure or expectations. It will never rush you, guilt you, or judge you. It assures us that even when it feels like the world is crumbling away, hope is always on the horizon, and all that we need to do is reach for it.

Pink calcite's calming effect makes it a favorite among counselors and healers too, as it supports open and honest communication with others, including the self. It promotes self-acceptance and instills a sense of comfort and contentment. If anxiety and stress are preventing you from processing and releasing emotional pain, use this crystal to soothe your heart and let go of any pent-up feelings. For those who need a little extra support in their healing process, pink calcite is an excellent choice.

Chakra:
Heart

Affirmation:
I honor and acknowledge my emotions, allowing them to flow through me without judgment or resistance.

Ritual: When uncomfortable feelings arise, meditate with pink calcite. Hold this crystal in your hand and let your body relax. Know that you are safe and supported. Tune in to your heart and give yourself permission to feel, releasing resistance. Notice the emotions that bubble up and observe them without judgment. Take a moment to pause and acknowledge that they are a passing experience rather than a reflection of who you are.

GARNET

Garnet is the real deal when it comes to devotion. Known for its regenerative qualities, garnet boasts a number of physical benefits, such as increased vitality, libido, and endurance. It gives you that extra oomph of energy to go the distance. This makes garnet an excellent crystal for those who have trouble motivating themselves consistently, as it instills a sense of discipline that helps in seeing tasks through to completion. Want to establish an exercise routine that you'll actually stick with, or tie up that project you've been promising to get to? This stone has got you covered.

Garnet is a powerful ally in matters of the heart. It has the ability to move a partnership on to the next stage of development, no matter what that might be. For relationships that have lost their spark, this crystal can be a lifesaver, helping to rekindle connection and deepen intimacy. A stone of passion and loyalty, it rejuvenates the heart center and strengthens feelings of love toward ourselves and others. By removing inhibitions and taboos, this stone helps us feel more comfortable and confident in expressing our true feelings and gives us the courage to take up space. It also weeds out toxic emotions like jealousy, mistrust, and hatred that may hinder our capacity to fully love.

Chakra:
Root, sacral, heart

Affirmation:
I am fully committed to achieving my goals and have the discipline needed to succeed.

Ritual: Set an intention to ground your focus with garnet. Choose a specific affirmation that you would like to work with, such as, "I am rooted in my strength and grounded in my purpose." Hold the garnet in your hand and repeat your affirmation out loud or in your mind. Feel its energy amplifying your intention and anchoring it deep within you. Carry the garnet with you throughout the day as a reminder of your intention.

PINK TOURMALINE

Pink tourmaline is a stone of compassion, nurturing, and self-love. Like all varieties of tourmaline, it is incredibly grounding and protective, but due to its association with the heart chakra, it provides the added benefit of emotional healing. This crystal promotes all types of love, and encourages sympathy and kindness toward others, as well as better listening and understanding. This makes it perfect for humanitarian work, and a symbol of everlasting friendship. Though pink tourmaline teaches us how to give with an open heart, it reminds us that this shouldn't be at our own expense. After all, "you can't pour from an empty cup." When we give too much of ourselves without taking the time to replenish our emotional reservoir, we end up feeling exhausted and burnt out. This crystal shows us that it's important to recognize that taking care of ourselves isn't selfish, but essential if we want to be able to fully show up for others.

Another way to make sure our cup stays full is by setting boundaries. Saying "no" to things that don't align with our values or that drain our energy is a powerful act of self-care, and pink tourmaline helps us stand strong if our thoughts begin to waver. If you start to feel guilty, meditate with this stone for a few moments to release any pressure or expectations on yourself, and make a decision that is right for you.

Chakra:
Root, heart, crown

Affirmation:
In this moment, I choose to prioritize my needs. It's okay to put myself first.

Ritual: Heal your emotional body with pink tourmaline. Come to a comfortable seated position and hold the crystal in your hands, connecting to its restorative energy. Visualize a pink light glowing from within the stone and an empty cup in front of you. Now imagine the light pouring into and filling the cup with vibrations of love. Once the cup is full, envision yourself drinking it, allowing its renewing energy to nourish your heart and mend emotional wounds.

SELENITE

Selenite is a beautiful crystal that exudes a calming and serene energy, making it perfect for meditation and spiritual practices. Associated with the third eye and crown chakras, this stone is great for enhancing intuition and connecting with higher consciousness. Its gentle energy promotes a sense of tranquility and inner peace that helps to drown out the noise of the outside world, allowing one to focus on what's happening within.

Selenite is renowned for its powerful cleansing properties, both energetically and spiritually. Its pure white and translucent appearance reflects its ability to purify and uplift the energy around it. This crystal can be used to remove stagnant or negative energy from a person, space, or other stones, replacing it with positive, fresh energy. "Out with the old, in with the new," is certainly the motto of this gem, which makes it a wonderful tool to turn to when you're in need of an energetic reset. We all experience moments in our lives when we feel stuck, whether it's in our career or relationships. Sometimes we hit a wall or we become complacent with a situation. Whatever the case may be, selenite assists in clearing out mental clutter and removing any lingering attachments that are bogging us down. If you find your thoughts slipping to events from the past, use this stone to return to the present moment.

Chakra:
Third eye, crown

Affirmation:
I am surrounded by pure and positive energy. I am ready to release the past and invite fresh changes into my life.

Ritual: Use selenite to reset your energy whenever you're feeling sluggish. Hold the crystal in your hand and slowly move it over your body in alignment with the chakras (starting at the top of the head and finishing at the base of the spine). Notice how much lighter you feel. If you need additional cleansing, use the stone to trace around your body to remove any remaining negativity.

RUBY

If you're in the market for a stone that will set your heart ablaze, ruby is for you. This passionate gem is like a matchstick to your soul, igniting a fiery drive within you that will help make you feel more alive than ever before. Connected to the energy of the sun, it has been called the inextinguishable flame, and it certainly lives up to its name. A symbol of vitality and passion, ruby burns through sluggishness and melancholy moods with ease and supercharges the heart center. Furthermore, it said to have a strong aphrodisiac effect. If you feel closed off from experiencing pleasure or have trouble connecting to your emotions, use this stone to help get your blood pumping and become more attuned to your desires. Place a piece of it in the bedroom for an extra spark of excitement.

Ruby is also a great stone for emotional healing. This crystal is all about rebuilding trust and confidence. When destructive or self-sabotaging behaviors start to rear their ugly head, ruby is there to swoop in and help save us from negative patterns. Besides keeping bad thoughts at bay, ruby supports you in tapping into your sense of self-worth. This stone wants us to believe in ourselves, because when we do, we can accomplish anything we set our minds to.

Chakra:
Root, heart

Affirmation:
When I connect to my inner fire, I can accomplish anything.

Ritual: Gather a small jar or container and a couple of scraps of paper. On each piece of paper, write a positive affirmation or self-love statement, such as, "I am worthy of love." Place the ruby in the jar as a symbol of love and empowerment. Whenever you need a boost of self-love, take a moment to pick a paper from the jar and read the affirmation aloud.

CITRINE

Brighter days are always ahead when citrine is by your side. Commonly referred to as the light stone, citrine shines like a beacon of hope throughout dark times. Its cheerful rays radiate joy and happiness to every corner of life, casting away somber moods and negativity. Just looking at this stone can lift one's spirits, as it helps us see the sunshine behind the clouds. It reminds us that while we may not be able to control certain situations, we can control how we respond to them. When facing inner challenges, oftentimes a shift in attitude is all we need to improve an experience. Citrine's positive, upbeat energy will keep you from feeling overwhelmed and allow you to see things from a different, optimistic perspective.

Citrine is a powerhouse when it comes to knowing your worth and owning it. Favored for its abundance-boosting properties, this crystal shines a light on your inner talents and unique gifts. It boosts confidence levels by highlighting our abilities for all to see, even ones we may not be aware of. It reaffirms our faith in ourselves and gives us the courage to reach for the stars. When we feel confident about ourselves, and worthy of love, we emit a certain energy that attracts people, opportunities, and experiences that are in alignment with our desires. By working with citrine, we can open ourselves up to new possibilities and begin manifesting the life of our dreams.

Chakra:
Sacral, solar plexus, crown

Affirmation:
I am proud of who I am. My confidence is unmatched. I am worthy of all the love and success that comes my way.

Ritual: Cultivate abundance by keeping a piece of citrine in your wallet or purse. You can also put it in your office or workspace to attract financial opportunities. If you own a business, placing this stone inside or near your cash register can draw money to your door and promote career success.

60

SMOKY QUARTZ

When your inner world is turned upside down, smoky quartz is the friend you need. Calming and grounding, this stone serves as a trusty life raft that can help you weather any storm. Its connection to the root chakra helps you feel secure and steady, even when everything else around you is in chaos. Smoky quartz is one of the best crystals for stress relief, as it helps neutralize anxieties and worries before they have a chance to spiral out of control. It helps soothe frayed nerves and put a stop to all the nagging thoughts that keep you trapped in lower vibrations.

Beyond its grounding properties, smoky quartz has many cleansing benefits. It gently dissolves negative energy, transforming it into something positive and constructive. Think of it as an exfoliating scrub for the soul—one that leaves you feeling lighter, clearer, and refreshed. This is especially helpful when moving past limiting beliefs and insecurities. When we hold onto negative beliefs about ourselves, such as "I'm not good enough," or, "I don't deserve love," we create a self-fulfilling prophecy. These thoughts create an energy that repels love and influences the way that we interact with others. We might push people away or sabotage a connection before it has chance to develop. However, this is where smoky quartz really thrives. It settles the flittering thoughts that lead to fear and helps us let go of anything that is no longer serving us.

Chakra:
Root

Affirmation:
My past does not define my future. I release myself from negative patterns of thinking and cleanse myself of unwanted attachments.

Ritual: Dissolve confusion with smoky quartz. Use this crystal as a tool for scrying or divination to gain insights and clarity on a particular situation or question. Hold the crystal in your hand, allowing its purifying presence to cleanse your aura. Begin to gaze into the depths of the stone, focusing on your intention. After a few minutes, you may start to receive intuitive messages or see symbols or images that can guide you forward.

PINK CHALCEDONY

Ready to become the best version of yourself? Pink chalcedony is here to help. Known as the generosity stone, this crystal has a warm and charitable energy that amplifies feelings of compassion and hope. It is an exceptional stone for humanitarian work and community-building, as it aids in creating harmonious relationships and fostering deeper connections. It allows us to see the good qualities in other people, which in turn can inspire us to embody those qualities ourselves. By fostering a sense of interconnectedness, pink chalcedony supports us in recognizing that we are not alone in our struggles, and that we all have an important part to play in making the world a better place.

With its loving and nurturing energy, this crystal can support us in adopting a more selfless approach to life, moving away from a quid pro quo or ego-driven mindset and embracing an authentic spirit of giving. It invites us to let go of expectations and attachments to outcomes, allowing us to give freely without seeking anything in return. Ultimately, pink chalcedony welcomes us to act from a place of genuine care and concern for others without worrying that it will come at our own expense. By dissolving judgments and assumptions, this crystal enables us to be more empathetic and understanding of other people's experiences, even when they are different from our own.

Chakra:
Heart

Affirmation:
I joyfully give from the abundance of my heart, knowing that my actions create ripples of positivity in the world and within myself.

Ritual: *If you've been feeling jaded, cynical, or pessimistic, use pink chalcedony to cleanse your heart and restore your faith in love. Meditate with the stone in your hands for a few minutes, allowing it to absorb any regrets, resentments, or negative attachments. Once you've shifted all of these energies out of your body and into the stone, hold the crystal under running water to release them.*

AMAZONITE

When gazing at the majestic greenish-blue hue of amazonite, one can't help but feel at peace. Its color and texture are often likened to the calming waters of the Amazon River, from which it takes its name. Dubbed the peacemaker stone, it is known for its harmonizing properties and ability to enhance communication. This is a great stone to have around whenever conflict arises. Its soothing presence relaxes the mind, reducing anxiety and stress. If you frequently get tongue tied, this stone can help you speak your truth with ease. By encouraging open and honest expression, amazonite helps us articulate our thoughts and feelings with clarity and compassion, connecting us to our inner voice. Further, its balancing influence allows us to receive input from others with an open mind. With this stone, we are able to release judgments and biases and see different perspectives or sides of a situation that we hadn't previously considered before.

Amazonite is also a stone of hope. It dispels feelings of despair, replacing them with a sense of optimism and faith. This crystal eases restless thoughts and worries that can cloud our minds, helping us to see beyond current circumstances and envision a future filled with potential. When we connect with the energy of this stone, we are reminded that brighter days are ahead and that the hardships we are experiencing are only temporary.

Chakra:
Heart, throat

Affirmation:
I am at peace within myself and the world around me. I release all worries and fears. My mind is calm and my heart is open.

Ritual: Invoke tranquility with amazonite. Create affirmations that promote inner peace such as, "Peace flows through me," or, "My heart is a sanctuary of serenity," and write them on small pieces of paper. Place your crystal on top of the affirmations and let its soothing energy infuse them. Keep these affirmations in places where you'd like to cultivate more peace, or carry them with you for a calming effect.

HEMATITE

When you find yourself lost in a sea of emotions, use hematite to cast an anchor ashore. One of the first things you'll notice about this crystal is its immediate grounding effect. This is likely due to the fact that hematite is denser and harder than your average stone. Holding it in your hand is like holding a small piece of the earth, providing a sense of stability and calm. This powerful gem is known as the stone of the mind for its ability to sharpen focus and enhance mental clarity and willpower. It imparts a steely determination and unwavering dedication to whoever uses it, making it an excellent ally in the face of confusion and uncertainty. If you need to combat scattered thoughts or flighty tendencies, this stone will support you in directing your attention to where it needs to go, and help you stay firmly rooted in your power.

In regards to self-love, hematite works wonders when it comes to standing up for yourself. This stone is anything but a pushover, and its sturdy energy stops people-pleasing and codependency dead in their tracks. Like a protective cloak, this crystal holds strong against outside influences, and ensures we won't budge on our emotional needs. It teaches us that boundaries are healthy and that setting them is one of the most powerful acts of self-love we can accomplish.

Chakra:
Root, solar plexus

Affirmation:
I am rooted like a tree, firmly grounded in the present moment.

Ritual: Meditate with hematite to ground yourself. Stand up tall and plant both feet on the ground. Hold your crystal in your hands, feeling its anchoring energy flowing down through your body into the earth. Continue to strengthen your connection to the earth by envisioning roots growing down from your feet toward the planet's core. Speak your intention for grounding out loud, such as, "I honor my boundaries and protect my energy."

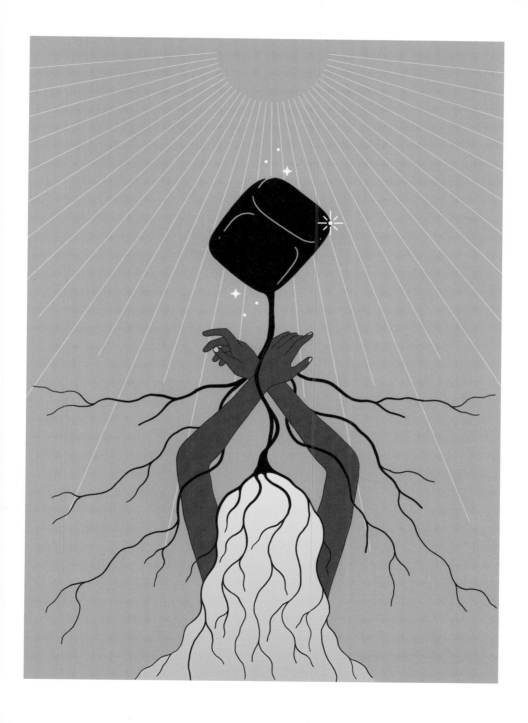

CLEAR QUARTZ

Known as the master healer of the mineral kingdom, clear quartz is unmatched in its versatility, helping to activate all seven chakras and infusing any situation with positivity. As its name suggests, clear quartz speaks to clarity of mind. When you're feeling overwhelmed and can't seem to focus, this crystal can help cut through mental fog and confusion. Its purifying energy filters out distractions and sweeps away competing thoughts clouding your mind. Due to its connection to the crown chakra, this crystal excels at helping you tap into higher states of consciousness and your divine purpose. It fosters a connection to spirit and to the universe at large. With greater awareness of your intentions, you'll be able to channel your energy in a positive direction.

Clear quartz is also a powerful amplifier. When placed near another crystal or object, it is said to amplify the energy of that object by resonating with its vibrations and intensifying its effects. The same applies to people too. Clear quartz magnifies the energy of our thoughts and intentions, and in doing so, helps us manifest our desires more quickly and effectively. This makes clear quartz a wonderful stone to have around if you seek to make positive changes in your life. Its cleansing properties will wash away any lingering negativity or limiting beliefs while its amplifying effects lend an extra surge of power and support to your goals.

Chakra:
All, but especially third eye and crown

Affirmation:
I trust in the infinite wisdom of the universe and welcome its guidance. My mind is clear and my soul is light.

Ritual: Get into a seated position on the ground. Hold your clear quartz crystal with both hands as you focus on your breath. On the inhale, visualize a white light entering your body through your nose, filling your lungs and chest with positive energy. As you exhale, envision tension and negativity leaving your body through your mouth as dark smoke. Continue this pattern until you feel completely relaxed and filled with light.

GREEN JADE

Green jade is a beautiful crystal that has been treasured for centuries for its healing properties, often serving as a protective talisman as well as a symbol of good luck. It has a strong connection to the heart chakra and is associated with harmony, love, peace, and serenity. One of its main benefits is its ability to help us break free from unhealthy relationships that drain our energy and cause emotional pain. It encourages us to let go of these toxic attachments and shift our focus and energy back to ourselves, and the relationships that nourish our heart and soul. By promoting independence and self-sufficiency, this crystal reminds us that we don't need anyone else to "complete" us or make us happy. We are whole, simply on our own.

Green jade is also helpful for dealing with inner turmoil, as its calming and cleansing properties help to soothe frayed nerves and dissolve negativity. Not only does it help us keep our cool throughout chaotic times, but it allows us to see situations clearly and objectively. This crystal excels at diffusing emotionally charged situations and supports us in tapping into our logical side. With this stone, we are able to gain a greater understanding of our own thoughts and patterns and come up with effective solutions for our problems.

Chakra:
Heart

Affirmation:
Where my attention goes, energy flows.

Ritual: Shield yourself against negativity by wearing green jade jewelry or keeping a piece in your pocket or purse. If you start to feel conflicted or uncertain about an issue, touch your crystal and take a deep breath to receive a surge of clarity. You'll instantly know whether something is or isn't in alignment with your desires, and be able to make a decision accordingly.

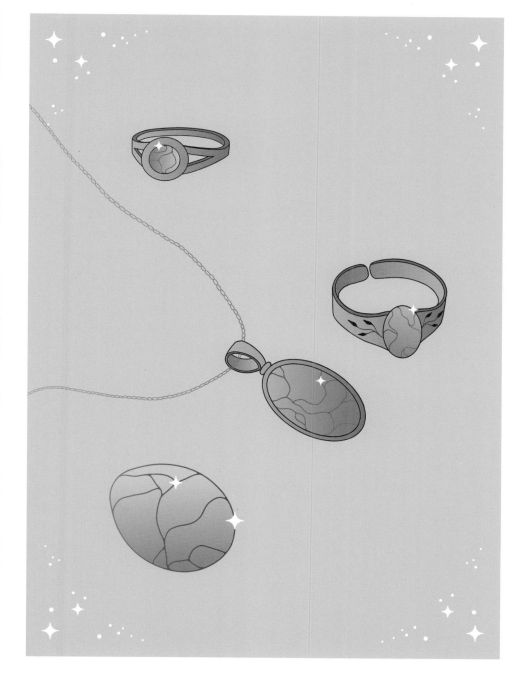

LEPIDOLITE

Have you ever felt like you're on an emotional rollercoaster? One moment you're up, the next you're down, and you just can't seem to find your footing. That's where lepidolite comes in. Dubbed the stone of transition, this crystal acts as a stabilizing force when navigating change, promoting inner peace and emotional balance. A go-to for post break up healing and stress relief, lepidolite helps us recognize when our emotions are spinning out of control and teaches us how to gently course-correct. Its serene energy calms the mind and soothes the nervous system, combating waves of overwhelm and returning us to our center. This stone is also said to ward off nightmares and insomnia, and is particularly good at putting an end to anxious or obsessive thoughts that keep us up at night. Like a sweet lullaby, this crystal sings us to sleep and melts our worries away.

Lepidolite moves us toward a vibration of self-love by encouraging us to take personal responsibility for our lives and the choices we've made. It invites us to be more honest and open with ourselves, and with others. By offering insights into the patterns and behaviors that are no longer serving us, this stone shows us the necessary steps we must take to transform our thoughts and create new, healthy habits.

Chakra:
Heart, third eye, crown

Affirmation:
I am at peace with my emotions. I am in control of my thoughts and reactions, and I choose to respond in healthy ways.

Ritual: If anxieties begin to cloud your mind, meditate with a lepidolite worry stone (a small smooth stone shaped like an oval, with a thumb-shaped indentation) or tumbled piece of lepidolite to soothe your soul. Hold the crystal in between your thumb and pointer finger, slowly massaging it back and forth. Allow its peaceful vibrations to dissolve stress.

TIGER'S EYE

Life has a tendency to throw us curveballs that can leave us feeling anxious and frazzled. From high-pressure work meetings to first dates, it's easy for our minds to get caught up in the moment and lose sight of the bigger picture. Sometimes we need to take a step back and ground ourselves before we can tackle the challenges that lie ahead. This is where the power of tiger's eye comes in handy. Tiger's eye is a fascinating crystal that comes in a variety of colors, but is most commonly found in shades of golden-brown with distinctive striped patterns. This stone has an earthy quality that brings focus, clarity, and stability to the mind. Whether you're facing a major decision or are simply feeling overwhelmed by the stresses of daily life, the grounding energy of this stone can help you find your center and regain your sense of calm.

Tiger's eye has many self-love benefits, but perhaps its biggest is its ability to help us harness our inner strength. This is the perfect stone to turn to in the face of adversity, as its motivating and courageous energy helps us conquer our fears and overcome hurdles. This crystal reminds us that we can handle anything that comes our way, and gives us the confidence to take action toward our goals. Use this stone to make choices that are in alignment with your values and stand by your convictions.

Chakra:
Root, sacral, solar plexus

Affirmation:
I am strong, courageous, and confident. I am determined to achieve my goals.

Ritual: Meditate with tiger's eye to tap in to courage. Place your feet firmly on the ground and stand tall. Hold tiger's eye over your solar plexus chakra (below your navel), as you repeat the affirmation, "I am a pillar of strength," aloud three times. You'll instantly feel your fears slip away as you embrace your personal power.

RED JASPER

While red jasper may look intense with its fiery red appearance, it's actually an incredibly nurturing stone. Aligned with the root chakra, this crystal is all about balance, and is unique in that it is both grounding and stimulating. So whether you need to crank up your energy levels, or dial them back, red jasper's got you covered. For those who feel sluggish or stagnant, this stone will help shake off lethargy and revitalize the soul. It adds fuel to one's desires and provides a spark of motivation. On the other hand, for those who feel scattered or distracted, this stone will help foster a strong connection with the earth, helping one feel more grounded and present in the physical world.

Red jasper also balances out aggressive energy. When we allow our emotions to build up without healthy outlets of expression, they can lead to red-hot tempers and outbursts that seem to come out of nowhere. In these instances, this crystal acts as a calming influence, helping to soothe and release pent-up energy in a more controlled and constructive matter. Not only that, but this gemstone promotes a deep sense of tranquility and wholeness. By connecting us to the earth's energies, it encourages us to align our actions and intentions with a greater sense of purpose and responsibility. It reminds us to channel our energy in positive and productive ways, rather than allowing it to manifest as aggression or confrontation.

Chakra:
Root

Affirmation:
With each breath, I let go of tension and invite emotional stability into my life. I am resilient, standing firm in the face of challenges.

Ritual: Use red jasper to cleanse and balance your energy field. Hold this crystal in one hand and pass it over your body starting from the top of your head and moving downward, visualizing the crystal absorbing any stagnant or negative energy. As you do this, set the intention of releasing any imbalances or tensions.

OBSIDIAN

When it comes to self-love, we can often become our own worst enemy, unknowingly creating obstacles that hinder our ability to truly embrace and nourish ourselves. We may engage in self-sabotaging behaviors or give into fear without even realizing it, and wonder why things never seem to work out the way we want them to. In these instances, obsidian can lend a helping hand. This crystal is a detoxifying and transformative stone that encourages introspection and growth. Through its piercing gaze, obsidian illuminates the shadows and cuts to the heart of whatever issue we're facing, increasing our self-awareness and empowering us to make conscious choices.

These reasons make obsidian an excellent choice for shadow work—a practice which involves exploring and integrating the unconscious and repressed aspects of ourselves. This stone serves as a mirror, reflecting our innermost thoughts, feelings, and fears back to us with clarity and honesty. If this process sounds daunting, don't worry. Obsidian is also a master of grounding. Its association with the root chakra gives it a stabilizing influence that will allow you to navigate uncomfortable emotions and memories with strength and resilience. By fostering a solid foundation, this stone helps you remain centered and courageous as you dive deep into the shadow realms of your psyche.

Chakra:
Root

Affirmation:
I embrace my shadows with courage and compassion, transforming them into sources of strength and wisdom.

Ritual: Carry a small piece of obsidian with you as a grounding talisman. You can keep it in your pocket, purse, or wear it as jewelry. If you're about to make an impulsive or self-destructive decision, hold this crystal in your hand to cultivate mindfulness and clarity. Consider if this is your higher self talking or your shadow side. Who will you choose to listen to?

BLUE SODALITE

Striking a balance between our head and our heart is no easy feat. The former represents logic and reason whereas the latter symbolizes emotions and intuition, and it's important to cultivate a connection to both. This is where blue sodalite shines. This crystal not only helps us in recognizing the value of our emotions and intuition, but encourages us to consider the practical aspects and consequences of our choices. For these reasons, blue sodalite has been dubbed both the logic stone and the poet's stone—as it supports critical-thinking and creative expression. Making decisions solely based on logic can cause us to suppress our true desires, but acting on pure feeling can lead us to make irrational, impulsive choices. This crystal teaches us that we must learn to integrate our intellectual and emotional capacities and find a harmonious alignment between our thoughts and our feelings.

Blue sodalite has the remarkable ability to help one speak their truth. This stone stimulates the throat chakra and enhances communication and self-expression, allowing us to voice our feelings without fear. By encouraging honest introspection, this stone enables us to recognize our strengths, weaknesses, and areas for growth and leads to greater self-awareness. If you have trouble standing up for yourself, this crystal can assist with setting healthy boundaries and asserting yourself in a confident manner.

Chakra:
Throat

Affirmation:
I am open to exploring my inner truth. My voice matters and my words are powerful.

Ritual: Speak clearly and calmly with blue sodalite. Meditate with this stone before any speaking engagements, difficult conversations, or negotiations. Hold the stone over your throat and breathe deeply. Envision a bright blue light glowing from the stone and passing through your throat, loosening your vocal cords and relaxing the muscles in your neck. Allow its soothing energy to melt through blockages as you focus on releasing tension from this area.

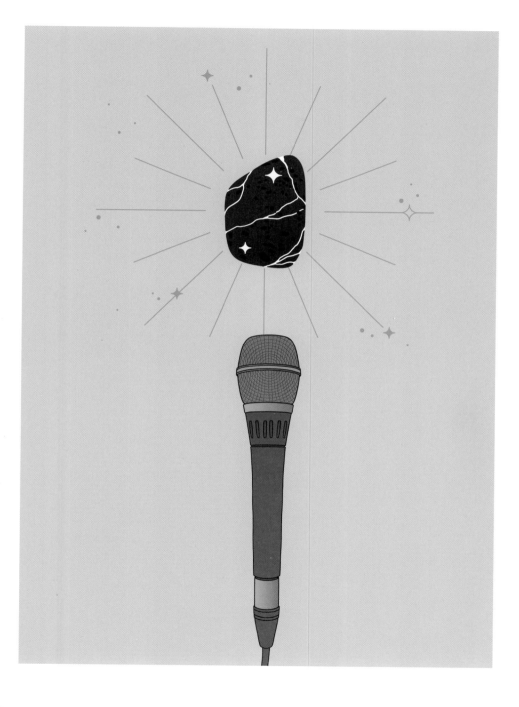

Now that you've learned all about crystals, it's time to put that knowledge to use. In this chapter, we'll be delving into the transformative power of our intentions and how we can combine them with the radiant energy of crystals to manifest our deepest desires and invite love into our lives. You see, the universe is an enchanting place, brimming with infinite possibilities. And at the heart of it all lies the immense power of our intentions. Our thoughts and wishes have the ability to shape our reality, and when we infuse them with focused intention, something extraordinary happens. It's like sending a love letter to the cosmos, and guess what? The universe is ready to deliver.

The following crystal spells, rituals, and meditations are designed to help you set powerful intentions for self-love, which will not only align you with the vibrational frequency of what you desire, but create an internal shift that fosters personal growth and healing. From creating love-inspired altars and crystal grids, to practicing heart-opening meditations, you'll discover how to unlock the secrets of crystal magick and infuse your life with unconditional love.

While the spells, rituals, and meditations may call for specific crystals, herbs, or items to be used, feel free to modify them as needed. If you're missing an item, simply swap it out for one with similar energetic properties, or omit it altogether. If you're unsure of what to use, general substitutions are as follows: clear quartz can be used in place of any stone, rosemary for any herb or plant, rose for any flower, and white candles for any other color candle.

SPELLS, RITUALS, & MEDITATIONS

HOW TO BUILD A SELF-LOVE ALTAR

The act of creating and tending to an altar can be a meditative and transformative practice that allows your relationship with love to thrive. Simply put, an altar is a sacred space used to cultivate a connection with your inner self. It serves as a focal point for meditation or energy work, and can be dedicated to any intention you desire.

Altars come in many shapes and sizes, but typically include a flat surface, such as a table or shelf, where various items can be placed. Your altar can be big or small, fancy or simple, traditional or unconventional—it's completely up to you. There is no one-size-fits-all approach when it comes to building an altar; what's important is that it looks and feels authentic to you and your unique needs.

Materials:

Paper and pen (optional)
Incense (optional)
Matches or a lighter
A cloth or mat
Rose quartz
White or pink candles
Fresh or dried lavender buds or rose petals
Heart-shaped items
Statue or photo of a love goddess

Directions:

Find a location in your home that feels special to you. It should be a place where you can sit or stand comfortably and remain undisturbed.

Gather the materials for your altar. You can add items that make you feel happy and uplifted, or personal tokens that inspire love.

Cleanse your materials of any negative energy they may have picked up. You can do this through smoke cleansing by wafting lit incense (any scent) around each item, or leaving them in the sunlight or moonlight for a few hours.

Now begin arranging your altar. Lay a cloth or mat on your chosen surface. Then, arrange the other materials in a way that feels harmonious and pleasing to you. If you chose to write down your self-love intention, add it to the altar. As always, follow your intuition.

Spend at least five to ten minutes each day sitting or standing in front of your altar. Hold your crystal and breathe deeply as you repeat your original intention. Allow loving vibrations and waves of compassion to fill you up. You'll find that the more room that you make for love, the more easily it will flow into your life.

Leave your altar up as long as you like, or until you feel your self-love intention is fulfilled.

> In regards to the specific items and their arrangement, pick ones whose energetic properties support self-love. In general, this may include elements such as crystals, candles, herbs, flowers, incense, statues, symbols, and other items that hold a spiritual or personal significance.

HOW TO ENCHANT JEWELRY & CHARMS

Turn everyday objects into powerful talismans and amulets through enchantment. The process of enchantment involves infusing pieces of jewelry or other wearable items (such as pins, keychains, coins, or personal tokens) with magickal energy or intentions to enhance their purpose and create a connection between the wearer and the desired outcome. While talisman and amulets are both worn for magickal purposes, they serve two very different purposes. Talisman are used to draw in or attract a desired energy or intention, while amulets are used to ward off or repel certain energies or influences.

You can program your favorite objects to support any intention you desire, such as health, protection, love, prosperity, and more. When choosing an object to enchant, consider that each crystal, metal, and symbol all have their own meanings and magickal associations. For instance, a jade necklace could be used as a talisman to call in abundance, a gold bracelet to manifest success, or a crescent moon pendant to harness one's intuition. Likewise, an obsidian ring could be worn as a protective amulet to guard against negative energy.

Materials:
Piece of jewelry or wearable charm
Incense
Matches or lighter
Clear quartz (optional)

Directions:
First, establish if your piece of jewelry or wearable charm will be a talisman (to draw something toward you) or amulet (to ward something off). Next, select an appropriate time to charge and enchant the item. For instance, Thursdays are ideal for making talismans, since this day is ruled by Jupiter, the planet of luck. If you're uncertain of what day or time to choose, simply follow your intuition and trust your gut. Once the timing is right, cleanse your jewelry and sacred space by lighting the incense and wafting its smoke around the item and room.

Come to a comfortable seated position and hold the jewelry in your hands. Focus on your intention and visualize the purpose or desired outcome you want the jewelry to assist you with. Hold this image in your mind's eye and let your energy pour into the item for as long as you can (ten to fifteen minutes if possible). When you feel that the jewelry has been fully infused with your energy, speak a simple affirmation aloud to support your intention and complete the enchantment, such as, "I attract love," or, "I am safe." Your jewelry is now ready. Whenever you want to receive a boost of power from the item or recharge your intention, hold it to your body so that it makes contact with your skin and repeat your affirmation out loud. To amplify your intentions even further, place the jewelry on or near clear quartz for a few hours, which will focus and strengthen the energies within the jewelry.

HEART HEALING RITUAL BATH

When your heart needs mending, turn to the healing power of rose quartz. Ritual baths work by combining the physical act of bathing with intention and energy work. Water is a powerful element that can help to cleanse and purify not only the physical body, but also the mind and spirit. When combined with other elements such as crystals, herbs, essential oils, and candles, a ritual bath can become a source of relaxation, healing, and change. This ritual bath is designed to gently soothe the emotional body and provide a safe space for the heart to heal. Infused with rose quartz—a stone of unconditional love, compassion, forgiveness, and self-acceptance—this bath helps wash away old emotional wounds as well as the pain of the past. Allow yourself to be held and supported by its nourishing waters as love fills you and surrounds you, restoring your heart to full health.

Materials:
Candle
Matches or lighter
Calming music (optional)
1 cup (240 g) of pink Himalayan coarse salt
5 drops of jasmine essential oil
2 tbsp of rose petals (fresh or dried)
Rose quartz

Directions:
Set the mood for your ritual by creating a peaceful and relaxing atmosphere. Dim the lights, light your candle, and play some calming music if you desire.

Fill your tub with warm water, then add the salt, essential oils, and rose petals. Take a few moments to center yourself and focus on an intention for healing your heart. This could be something like, "I invite healing and love into my heart," or, "I release any pain or hurt I am carrying in my heart."

Once you've decided, hold your rose quartz over your heart and set your intention by saying it aloud. Then, add the crystal to the water, allowing it to infuse the bath with its healing energy. Step into the tub and as you soak in the bath, visualize the rose quartz filling your body with its gentle, loving energy, extending to the deepest corners of your heart. You can also hold the crystal to your chest to melt away deeper aches and pains.

When you're done, drain the tub and watch the water carry all your worries away, then carefully snuff out the candles. After your bath, take some time to reflect on your experience. Write in your journal or simply sit in silence and bask in the loving energy that surrounds you.

COLOR MAGICK MANICURE

This DIY manicure taps in to the power of color magick, a practice that harnesses the energy and symbolism associated with different colors to set and amplify intentions.

Here are a few associations and meanings connected to various colors:

Red: *Energy, passion, love, strength, courage, determination, excitement*

Orange: *Joy, creativity, pleasure, vitality, success, confidence, motivation*

Yellow: *Intellect, happiness, clarity, optimism, positivity, hope*

Green: *Abundance, growth, healing, balance, luck, fertility, harmony*

Blue: *Trust, communication, peace, stability, wisdom, loyalty*

Purple: *Intuition, psychic abilities, spirituality, independence*

Pink: *Love, romance, nurturing, kindness, compassion, friendship*

Black: *Protection, banishing, grounding, release, power, control*

White: *Purity, clarity, new beginnings, virtue, innocence*

Brown: *Stability, grounding, strength, comfort, structure*

Gray: *Balance, neutrality, diplomacy, maturity, compromise*

Materials:
Nail cutters
Nail file
Nail polish
Clear quartz

Directions:
Start with clean, polish-free hands. Cut, file, and shape your nails to your liking. Select a nail polish color that represents the energy you wish to manifest. Hold the clear quartz crystal and bottle of nail polish in your hands, cupping them together so they touch. Take a few deep breaths, then bring your intention to the forefront of your mind, using the energy of clear quartz to sharpen your focus. For instance, this could be something like, "My mind is calm and my body is relaxed," if you're working with blue polish, or, "I am surrounded by love," for pink polish. Speak your intention aloud or to yourself a few times, allowing the amplifying effects of clear quartz to increase its power. Continue to do this as you focus on infusing your intention into the nail polish.

Once you feel that the nail polish has been sufficiently charged, start painting your nails. As you apply each coat, visualize the energy of your intentions soaking into your nails, boosting their power. I recommend applying at least two coats of polish for even color and a clear top coat for extra protection if you desire. Remember to go slow and enjoy the process. Now whenever you catch a glimpse of your nails throughout your day, you'll be reminded of the intentions you've set.

CRYSTAL ELIXIR FOR BREAKING BAD HABITS

Nip bad habits in the bud with this amethyst-infused crystal elixir. A crystal elixir, also know as a gemstone elixir, is a liquid preparation that harnesses the energy and properties of crystals. It is created by placing crystals in or around water to allow their essence to infuse into the liquid. The water absorbs the vibrational energy and qualities of the crystals, producing a potent elixir that can be ingested or used topically.

Sometimes bad habits can develop into toxic patterns that prevent us from experiencing the love we deserve. Breaking a bad habit can be a challenging task because our habits are deeply ingrained patterns of behavior. To do so requires a combination of awareness, intention, and discipline. That's where amethyst comes in. This crystal has a strong "sobering" effect on negative influences and attachments, purifying the mind and body of unwanted energies. It also enhances intuition and the ability to connect with our higher selves. With this stone, we are able to curb impulsive tendencies, resist temptation, and act in accordance with our best interests.

You can modify this elixir for other intentions by using different crystals in place of amethyst, but please check the stones you use are water-safe.

Materials:
Amethyst
Purified water
Clean glass or jar
Notepad and pen

Directions:
Prepare for the ritual by rinsing your piece of amethyst in clean water to remove any dirt or residue, then place it to the side. Begin by setting an intention to break a specific bad habit that you want to release. Write it down in the notepad. Fill the glass or jar with purified water. Place your crystal inside the jar. Set the jar in a place where it will receive moonlight for several hours. You can leave it overnight or for a minimum of six hours. While the elixir is charging in the moonlight, take some time to meditate or reflect on your intention. Visualize yourself free from this habit and the positive emotions associated with this release. What will your life look like without it? How will it feel?

After the elixir has charged in the moonlight, remove the amethyst from the water. Your elixir is now ready to be consumed. You can keep it in your current glass, transfer it to a water bottle, or divide it up into several smaller dropper bottles. Drink the elixir throughout the day, allowing its cleansing properties to wash away toxic ties and energetic blockages throughout your body and spirit. As you sip the elixir, repeat your intention in your mind, imagining yourself breaking the habit and following your intuition.

PLANT MAGICK SPELL FOR PERSONAL GROWTH

Allow the seeds of your intentions to flourish with the abundance-boosting properties of green aventurine and plant magick. Green aventurine is often associated with growth, renewal, and good fortune. Its vibrant green color represents the energy of nature and the vitality of life. As a symbol of growth, it carries the essence of new beginnings, fresh opportunities, and the potential for personal transformation. Plant magick, also known as herbal magick, is the practice of using plants and herbs for their spiritual and magickal properties. It involves harnessing the energy and essence of plants to aid in manifestation and healing. While this spell incorporates plants, don't be intimidated if you don't have a green thumb! No prior plant experience is necessary. All that is required is a willingness to evolve and the courage to tap into your heart's desires.

Materials:
Matches or lighter
White candle
Green aventurine
Small bowl of soil or potting mix
Small potted plant or sprig of fresh greenery
  (such as basil or mint)
Watering can or spray bottle filled with water

Directions:
Light the white candle and take a few deep breaths to center yourself. Hold the green aventurine in your hand and close your eyes. Envision yourself surrounded by a green light that symbolizes growth, vitality, and abundance. Visualize the light flowing into your body and filling you up with fresh energy.

Hold the small bowl of soil or potting mix and hold it in your hands. Speak your intention for personal growth using affirming and positive language. For example, "I am open to learning and growing in every area of my life. I am ready to embrace new opportunities and expand my horizons." Gently place the potted plant or greenery into the bowl of soil. If using a potted plant, you may need to dig a small hole to make room for its roots. Pat down the soil around the base of the plant to secure it.

Hold the green aventurine over the plant or greenery. Visualize its energy bathing the soil and nourishing the plant. Imagine that you are planting the seeds of your intention and that they will grow and thrive over time. Use the watering can or spray bottle to water the plant, saying a silent affirmation. The water will carry your intention deep into the roots of the plant and spread throughout its leaves and stems.

Sit in silence for a few moments and reflect on the ritual. When you feel ready, extinguish the candle and give thanks for the opportunity to connect with nature and cultivate personal growth. As you tend to the potted plant or greenery's needs every day, you'll be invited to check in with yourself and your progress.

SELF-LOVE SPELL JAR

Let the magick of self-acceptance and inner beauty intertwine with this self-love spell jar. This spell jar serves as a vessel for our deepest affirmations and acts as a constant reminder of our innate value. It is a sacred space where we infuse the power of crystals, herbs, and intentions to nourish our souls and cultivate a genuine love for who we are.

This spell jar is designed to help you align your thoughts, emotions, and actions with the energy of self-love. When completed, it becomes a tangible representation of your commitment to prioritizing self-care, practicing self-compassion, and cultivating a positive self-image. Remember that the spell jar is a personal and sacred creation, infused with your own intentions and energy, so feel free to modify the ingredients so that they resonate with you.

Materials:
Candle
Incense
Small glass jar or bottle with a tight lid
Pink Himalayan salt
A couple of pinches of dried lavender buds
A couple of pinches of dried rose petals
Rose quartz
Citrine
Clear quartz
White or brown sugar
Pink ribbon or string

Directions:
Begin in a calm space where you can focus. Light your incense with your pre-lit candle and cleanse your space and tools. Take a few deep breaths, close your eyes, and connect with your heart center. Visualize a warm pink light surrounding you. Assemble your ingredients. Hold each item in your hands, envisioning it radiating love, compassion, and self-acceptance. As you add each ingredient, speak affirmations of self-love and acceptance, such as: "I am a fierce and radiant being, worthy of love and all the blessings life has to offer." You can also write them down if you wish. Begin layering the ingredients into the small glass jar or bottle, one by one. Start with a base layer of pink Himalayan salt to remove energetic blocks. Add a couple of pinches of dried lavender buds for relaxation and peace, and a couple of pinches of dried rose petals for beauty and harmony. Place the rose quartz, citrine, and clear quartz inside the jar to promote love, happiness, and clarity. Sprinkle a small amount of sugar over the crystals to symbolize sweetening your self-perception.

Close the jar tightly, sealing the loving energy within. Take the pink ribbon or string and tie it around the neck of the jar. As you do so, visualize this ribbon as a symbol of self-love, securing the intentions you've set. Hold the jar in your hands and give it a gentle shake to activate its power. Place the jar on your altar, nightstand, or any space where you can see it regularly. Whenever you need a boost of self-love, revisit the jar and renew your intention to take care of your mind, body, and spirit.

NEW MOON CRYSTAL GRID

Every new moon offers an opportunity for a fresh start. The new moon is associated with new beginnings because it marks the start of a new lunar cycle. This is a time of darkness and introspection, where we can shift our focus inward and reflect on our goals for the upcoming cycle.

This ritual will teach you how to harness the power of the new moon by creating a crystal grid. A crystal grid is an arrangement of stones that are placed in various patterns (typically using sacred geometry) for the purpose of amplifying the stones' energies and intentions. The patterns can range from simple to complex, and many pre-printed layouts can be found online. You can also create your own pattern based on your intuition.

For this ritual, we will be using the "Seed of Life" pattern which supports new cycles and personal growth. It works with thirteen crystals since the number thirteen has a strong link to lunar energy, though you are free to modify the number of stones to your liking.

Materials:
- Flat surface to create your grid (such as a table or cloth)
- Matches or lighter
- Incense
- Small piece of paper and pen
- 1 large selenite
- 3 medium moonstone
- 3 medium green aventurine
- 3 small clear quartz
- 3 small labradorite

Directions:
Cleanse your space and crystals of negative energy by lighting the incense and wafting its smoke around the room and each stone. Reflect on what you'd like to call in during this lunar phase and formulate an intention. For example, you could use, "I am open to the magick of new beginnings. I am filled with hope, renewal, and inspiration." Write your intention down on a small piece of paper.

Place the paper in the middle of your cloth or table. This marks the center of your crystal grid. With your intention in mind, begin arranging the stones, laying the selenite on top of the paper first. Continue by creating a small circle around the selenite with alternating moonstone and green aventurine crystals. Then place the remaining clear quartz and labradorite crystals in a larger circle along the outer edges of the grid, alternating between the two types.

Now it's time to activate your grid. Point your finger and imagine a white light beaming from its tip. Begin to draw an invisible line between each stone with your finger until all the stones are connected in light. Your grid is now ready for use. Spend time near it every day to deepen meditation, cleanse your aura, and renew your intentions. I recommend leaving the grid up for the duration of the lunar cycle (one month) or until whenever you feel that your intention has been manifested. When you're finished with the grid, remove the stones in reverse order to close out the practice.

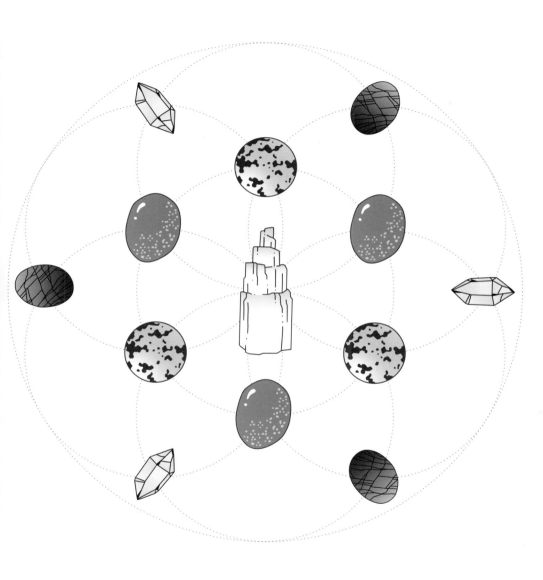

INNER BEAUTY MIRROR SPELL

Cultivate a positive self-image and let your beauty radiate from the inside out with this mirror spell. The mirror serves as a reflective surface, allowing us to see ourselves more clearly, both physically and energetically. When we cast a mirror spell with the intention of self-empowerment and self-acceptance, we open the door to transforming our self-perception and embracing our inherent beauty and worth.

> *To ensure the effectiveness of this spell, it is crucial that you do not allow any negative thoughts or energy to distract your focus as you gaze at yourself in the mirror. While it can be easy for insecurities and doubts to creep in during this process, it is important that you maintain a positive mindset. Refrain from giving attention or energy to any perceived flaws or imperfections. Instead, redirect your focus toward embracing the positive aspects and qualities you love about yourself.*

Materials:
Mirror
Red or pink candles
Matches or lighter
Garnet
Red or pink lipstick or chapstick
Perfume (optional)

Directions:
Find a quiet space where you can cast the spell without distractions. Set up your mirror in front of you, and place the red or pink candles on either side to invoke desire and self-love. Light the candles and turn off or dim all other lights. Hold the garnet crystal in your hands, feeling its fiery and passionate energy warming your palm. Garnet is a stone of commitment, so let its motivating presence inspire devotion toward your intention to embrace your inner beauty. Now gaze into the mirror as you slowly apply the red or pink lipstick or chapstick. Take your time and relish the process as you admire yourself. Feel free to put on your favorite slow song to slip into a sensual mood. Allow yourself to truly see and connect with your reflection. Remember, this is a sacred space for positive energy, so if you find your attention slipping toward a feature you dislike, gently bring your focus back to something you appreciate about yourself.

Once you feel empowered and ready to move forward with your intention, softly whisper the following aloud three times: "In this mirror's reflection, I clearly see, my beauty shining brilliantly." Seal the spell by kissing the mirror or spritzing some of your favorite perfume on your wrists and neck. You can continue to perform this spell for another two days if you wish, each time lighting the same candles until they've completely burned down.

FORGIVENESS SPELL

Forgiveness doesn't always come easy, but rhodonite is here to open your heart to the process. Holding onto grudges and resentment not only keeps us fixated on the past, but can damage our existing and future relationships. When we cling onto anger, resentment, and bitterness, it creates a cycle of negativity and mistrust that is difficult to break. However, rhodonite's compassion-boosting properties can help us release these negative feelings by bathing us in a current of kindness, empathy, and acceptance.

In this spell, you'll be invited to purify your heart center and let go of the pain that is weighing you down. By cultivating forgiveness, you'll be able to heal old emotional wounds and gain a better understanding of yourself and others. As you cast this spell, remember that forgiveness can take time, so don't pressure yourself to release everything in one sitting. If you still feel hurt, be gentle and set aside some time for another session. Continue to repeat this spell as often as needed to support your journey toward forgiveness.

Materials:
Matches or lighter
White candle
Rhodonite
Paper and pen
Fireproof bowl or dish

Directions:
Find a space to perform the ritual where you won't be disturbed, removing any flammable objects from the area. Light the white candle and place it in front of you. Hold the piece of rhodonite in your hands and take a few deep breaths to quiet your mind and relax your body. Close your eyes and bring to mind the person or situation you need to forgive. Allow yourself to feel any emotions that come up, but don't let them distract your focus. Make room to honor the emotions without letting them carry you away.

Now visualize the person or situation surrounded by a soft pink light, symbolizing compassion and forgiveness. Take the pen and paper and write down any negative thoughts or feelings that you've been holding onto regarding the person or situation. Be honest with yourself and don't hold back. Once you've finished writing, take the paper and hold it over the candle flame, allowing it to burn and release the negative energy. Transfer the lit paper to a fireproof bowl or dish. As it continues to burn, hold your rhodonite crystal to your heart, repeating the following affirmation: "I am filled with unconditional love. I choose to forgive. I am free from the past." Hold the crystal for a few minutes, allowing its tender energy to dissolve any blockages around your heart. When you are ready, extinguish the candle and notice how much lighter your heart feels.

GODDESS GLOW GUA SHA FACIAL

Flush away negative energies and improve skin health with this relaxing and detoxifying facial. This beauty ritual combines the healing properties of jade with the therapeutic benefits of gua sha to give you the ultimate glow. Gua sha is a traditional Chinese healing technique that involves scraping a smooth-edged tool along the skin to stimulate blood flow and promote healing. The tool is typically made of stone, like jade or rose quartz.

Gua sha is known to have many benefits, such as improving circulation, relieving muscle tension, and reducing inflammation. Energetically, gua sha is an amazing tool for sloughing off all the stagnant energies and limiting beliefs that are preventing you from loving yourself. As you perform this ritual, imagine scraping away any past insecurities to reveal the radiant and confident you that has always been there.

There are a few rules about gua sha you should know before you begin. All movements should be upward and follow lymphatic flow. Repeat each movement three to five times before moving on to the next area of your skin. Lastly, gua sha is not recommended for those with sunburns, rashes, or blood coagulation issues.

Materials:
Your favorite cleansing and toning products
Skin serum or facial oil
Gua sha tool (preferably jade or rose quartz)
Mirror

Directions:
Start by cleansing and toning your face in accordance with your usual skincare routine. Apply a few drops of your favorite skin serum or facial oil to your neck and face. Using the long, inward curved side of the gua sha tool, begin sweeping up the side of the neck, starting at the collarbone and moving toward the jawline. Repeat on the other side. Position the gua sha tool on its side so that the "heart" portion frames the jawline. Glide it from the center of the chin out towards the ears. Repeat on the other side. Using the longest side of the tool, massage the cheekbones. Start above the mouth and to the side of the nose, dragging the tool upward along the cheekbones to the temples. Repeat on the other side. With the longest curve of the "heart" place the tool flat against the inner corner of the eye and move out towards the temples (this is a delicate area, so I suggest using a lighter hand). Repeat on the other side. Finally, move up to the forehead, using the longest side of the gua sha to scrape from above the eyebrows up toward the hairline. Repeat this on the other side.

Finish the ritual by applying the rest of your skincare products and reflecting on how you feel. Gaze in the mirror and admire your new glow.

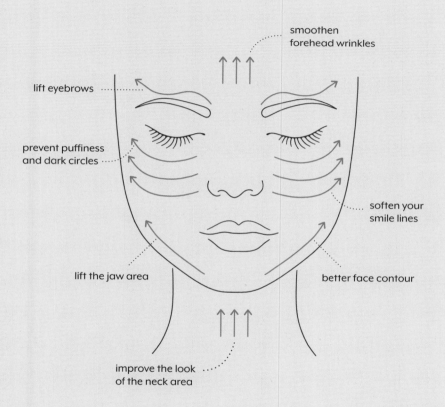

smoothen
forehead wrinkles

lift eyebrows

prevent puffiness
and dark circles

soften your
smile lines

lift the jaw area

better face contour

improve the look
of the neck area

CORD-CUTTING RITUAL

Cut toxic ties once and for all with this liberating ritual. A cord-cutting ritual is a spiritual practice that aims to sever the energetic ties or "cords" that we may have with people, places, or things that no longer serve our highest good. While this practice is frequently used with relationships, it can also help with fears, addictions, or other traumas. The cords here are not physical but rather symbolic of the emotional and energetic connections we have with these aspects of our lives. Cutting these cords enables us to release the emotional baggage and energy blockages that are keeping us stuck in old patterns and reclaim our power.

This ritual harnesses the power of obsidian to banish unwanted influences. Known for its detoxifying and protective properties, this stone is a pro at drawing out hidden fears and repressed feelings so that they can be released. While obsidian isn't a particularly hard crystal, it is capable of being very sharp—even sharper than surgical steel! However, due to its brittle nature, this stone is better at cutting in a metaphorical rather than literal sense. If obsidian isn't available to you, use another black stone in its place, such as black tourmaline or onyx.

Materials:
Obsidian

Directions:
Come to a seated position and hold the obsidian in your hands. Allow its grounding presence to filter out distractions and bring your mind to a state of quiet contemplation. Take a few deep breaths and relax your body. Once you feel settled and connected to your truth, think of the thing you want to release, whether it be a person, situation, habit, or belief. Visualize it in front of you, along with a cord connecting you both. See the cord in as much detail as possible. It may appear as a string, wire, chain, ribbon, or rope. Notice its color, texture, thickness, and where it's attached to your body. It's common for cords to attach to the chakras, so paying attention to those points may give you insight into the energetic nature of the connection. For instance, a cord located at the throat chakra might suggest that a connection is hindering your ability to express yourself freely.

Now it's time to cut the cord. Grab your piece of obsidian and make a strong, horizontal cutting motion through the cord as you repeat the following out loud: "I release you and I set myself free." Visualize the cord being permanently severed and the threads disappearing. Make sure to fill your heart with love and gratitude as you do this, as releasing a cord in anger will only strengthen the connection between you. After you cut the cord, notice the energy shift in your body as your power flows back to you.

CRYSTAL ELIXIR FOR BOOSTING CONFIDENCE

Have you ever found yourself doubting your abilities, questioning your decisions, or feeling like an imposter in your own life? If so, this confidence-boosting elixir is just what you need. Drawing upon the vivacious and inspiring energies of carnelian, this elixir is the perfect remedy for shaking off insecurities and bolstering self-esteem. Carnelian is one of the best crystals for building self-confidence, as it stimulates the root, sacral, and heart chakras. When these chakras are brought into alignment, we feel physically grounded, emotionally open, and spiritually empowered in our lives.

Carnelian is safe to use in distilled water. However, please refrain from using it in saltwater, as saltwater can damage its surface. If you don't have carnelian on hand, swap it for a stone with similar properties, but make sure it is water-safe and non-toxic. Many stones contain trace elements that can be harmful when ingested, so don't skip this step. I recommend citrine and clear quartz as safe alternatives.

Materials:
Carnelian
Clear glass jar or bottle
Purified or filtered water
Red, orange, or yellow flowers (optional)

Directions:
Cleanse your carnelian by holding it under running water for a few minutes. Make sure it is free of dirt and debris. Fill your glass jar or bottle with purified or filtered water. Place the carnelian in the jar in a sunny spot to charge for several hours or overnight, allowing the carnelian to infuse the water with its energy. If desired, surround the jar with bright flowers that represent confidence and self-love, like sunflowers, daffodils, or roses.

Once the water has been infused, remove the carnelian and take a moment to focus on your intention for confidence. Hold the jar or bottle of water in your hands and speak your intention out loud. You can say something such as, "I am confident, strong, and a force to be reckoned with." Take small sips of the elixir and feel its empowering essence surging through your body and revitalizing your spirit. If your mind starts to wander toward negative thoughts or doubts, take another sip of the elixir and repeat your affirmation again. Continue this process until you feel completely filled with confidence.

Close out the ritual by taking a few minutes to reflect on all the amazing things that make you uniquely you. If you have leftover elixir, you can drink the remainder throughout the day, or add it to baths, teas, or other spells for a boost of confidence.

FULL MOON RELEASE RITUAL

The full moon is a time of release, transformation, and clarity. It represents a culmination, completion, and fruition of the energy and intentions that were set during the new moon. As the moon reaches its fullest point, it symbolically illuminates the shadows and hidden aspects of ourselves and our lives, bringing them to the surface for us to acknowledge and release. Harnessing the potent energy of this lunar phase can help us gain clarity on what we need to let go of (such as old patterns, behaviors, or ways of thinking) and allow us to move forward in our journey of self-love.

In addition to the full moon, this ritual draws upon the purifying properties of malachite and bay leaves to support your intentions. Malachite is a powerful heart chakra stone that flushes out emotional blockages and negativity. It provides the insight needed for personal growth as well as the capacity to embrace change. Bay leaves are widely known as a symbol of protection, courage, and strength. They are often incorporated into cleansing rituals in order to remove unwanted energies from a person or space. Bay leaves also resonate with the solar plexus chakra, allowing you to harness your personal power and take responsibility for your life.

Materials:

Malachite
Pen
Bay leaves
Matches or lighter

White candle
Fireproof dish or
    container

Directions:

Start by meditating with malachite. Hold the crystal in your hands and close your eyes. Feel its transformative energy slowly opening your heart to change and casting away any fears. Let it fill you with a sense of courage and a desire to step outside your comfort zone. Once you feel ready, begin to think about the intention you'd like to set for this ritual—what past events, emotions, or patterns do you want to release? Write them down one by one on the bay leaves using the pen. These could be things like "fear" or "a toxic relationship." You might use multiple bay leaves if there are several things you'd like to release, or just one if you're focusing on a single item. Regardless, take your time to reflect on each item and how it has affected you.

Light the white candle and place it in front of you. Hold the bay leaf over the candle flame until it catches fire (please exercise caution, as the bay leaf may crackle and split when lit), then repeat the following affirmation aloud: "I let go of all that no longer serves me." Carefully transfer the lit bay leaf to the fireproof dish or container to continue burning. As it burns, visualize the things you wrote down being released and disappearing from your life. Repeat this process with any remaining bay leaves. Once all the leaves have fully burned down and the ashes have completely cooled, hold the malachite over the dish. Visualize the negative energy being transmuted and released into the universe. Afterwards, sit in silence for a few minutes to express gratitude for the release and the space it has created for positive energy. Finish the ritual by snuffing out the candle.

SWEET DREAMS SPELL

Dreams are a wonderful tool for connecting with the inner self. They offer a window into the subconscious mind, where many of our deepest fears and desires reside. When we open ourselves to the magick of our dreams, we gain access to these inner realms along with a deeper understanding of the emotions and experiences that shape us. This understanding can be helpful in promoting self-love because it allows us to identify areas where we may need to nurture and care for ourselves more deeply.

Materials:
Paper and pen
Amethyst
Small bowl of water
1 tsp of dried lavender or a few drops of lavender essential oil

This spell will prepare you to receive dream insights by calming the mind and body and encouraging rest. Drawing upon the soothing properties of amethyst, this spell creates a tranquil atmosphere that melts away worries and stress. Perform this spell at least an hour before bedtime to allow yourself to fully unwind.

Directions:

Find a quiet place in your bedroom to perform the spell. Power down your phone and any other electronic devices so you won't be disturbed. Place the paper and pen next to your bed. Dim the lights and lie down. Hold the amethyst crystal in your hands and take a few deep breaths. Scan your body from head to toe to identify any areas of tightness or tension. For instance, are you furrowing your brow or clenching your jaw? Does your chest feel heavy or does your back feel stiff? Make a note of these areas.

With your crystal in hand, visualize a gentle and calming purple light emanating from the stone and surrounding you. Feel its soothing energy flowing through your mind and relaxing your muscles. Now envision the light surging to the parts of your body that are tense, washing over them in a healing current and dissolving all knots. Once you've worked through these areas, set the amethyst aside.

Open your eyes and come to a seated position. Place the small bowl of water in front of you. Add the dried lavender or a few drops of lavender essential oil to the bowl. Stir the water with your finger and visualize the scent of lavender filling the air around you, calming and soothing your senses. Close your eyes and take a deep breath in through your nose, inhaling the scent of lavender. Hold your breath for a few seconds, then exhale slowly through your mouth. Repeat this a few times until you feel completely at peace. If desired, you can repeat an affirmation to promote rest and dreams at this time, such as, "Every night, I drift into a deep sleep, awakening refreshed."

Finally, pick up the amethyst and place it under your pillow before going to bed to safeguard your dreams. In the morning, jot down your dreams using the paper and pen. Reflect on the symbols and imagery and allow your intuition to guide you toward their meaning.

SUN MEDITATION TO SUPERCHARGE THE HEART

Does your heart feel depleted or worn out? Restore it to its full power with this sun meditation. The sun is associated with strength, vitality, and life force energy, and can be a powerful source of spiritual renewal. Just as the sun nurtures life of earth, this meditation can be used to encourage positive transformation and personal growth. By harnessing the properties of the sun, you'll be able to supercharge your heart center and expand your capacity to give and receive love.

A sun meditation is a form of meditation that involves visualizing the sun and connecting to its energy in order to restore and nourish the spirit. It is typically done outdoors during sunny days, but can be performed inside near a window if preferred. It's best to choose a time when the sun is not at its peak to avoid excessive sun exposure. Make sure to apply an ample amount of sunscreen before spending time in the sun.

Materials:
Comfortable cushion or mat
Citrine

Directions:
Begin by finding a peaceful space to perform the ritual. If possible, choose a spot where you can bask in the sunlight or be near a sunny window. Sit comfortably on a cushion or mat with your spine straight and your hands resting on your knees. Take five deep breaths to center yourself. Hold the citrine crystal in your hands and close your eyes. Visualize yourself sitting in a beautiful field of sunflowers with the radiant sun shining down upon you. Feel its warmth on your skin as you focus on your heart center. Allow the sunlight to flow through your body, cleansing you of all negativity.

Now envision a bright, golden light emanating from your chest. Feel this light expanding and growing with every breath you take. As you continue to breathe deeply, hold the citrine up to the sunlight or near the sunny window so that it catches the light. Imagine the sunlight streaming through the crystal and infusing it with fresh energy. With each inhale, imagine the golden light from your heart center flowing into the citrine crystal and filling it with even more light and energy. As you exhale, imagine any negative or heavy emotions leaving your body and being replaced with this beautiful, golden light. Allow yourself to feel lighter, more open, and full of positivity. Continue to hold the citrine in your hands and bask in the sunlight for as long as you like. When you feel ready, slowly open your eyes and continue to move through your day with love and optimism.

HEALTHY BOUNDARIES SPELL

Learning how to set and maintain healthy boundaries is a crucial skill we must develop on our self-love journey. Boundaries are important because they allow us to recognize and honor our emotions, needs, and limits. By defining what is acceptable and what isn't, we are not only able to protect our energy and prioritize self-care, but make choices that are truly aligned with our values.

This spell uses the grounding influence of hematite to cast a circle of protection that will help you establish healthy boundaries. Hematite acts as an anchoring force, fortifying the mind and strengthening willpower. With this stone by your side, you'll be able to stand your ground and guard yourself against outside influences. If hematite is not available to you, I suggest using another grounding stone, like black tourmaline, smoky quartz, or bloodstone.

Materials:
Matches or lighter
Incense
Hematite

Directions:
Cleanse your space and tools by lighting incense and wafting the smoke throughout the area and around the hematite. Stand in the center of your space with your feet firmly planted on the ground. Take a few deep breaths, allowing yourself to become present and grounded. Visualize roots extending from the soles of your feet, connecting you with the earth. Hold the hematite and close your eyes. Feel its energy, weight, and coolness. Visualize any stagnant or negative energies being absorbed by the stone, purifying and aligning it with your intention. With your stone in hand, slowly walk clockwise around the perimeter of your space to cast a circle of protection. Visualize a bright, shimmering light extending from the stone. Repeat an affirmation that supports your intention, such as, "With hematite's might, I set my boundaries right."

Once you have completed the circle, return to the center of your space. Hold the stone in front of you and envision a powerful beam of light emanating from it, filling the circle until it is fully illuminated. As the light expands, affirm your personal intention for setting boundaries and establishing a protective space. You can say, "I am strong and worthy of respect. I honor my boundaries." Take a few moments to meditate or simply stand in the circle, allowing yourself to fully embody the sense of protection and empowerment it brings. To close the ritual, walk counterclockwise around the circle, envisioning the energy retracting back into the hematite stone. Carry the stone with you as a protective shield to reinforce your boundaries.

SPELL FOR RELEASING PERFECTIONISM

Have you ever noticed how we can be our own toughest critics? While it's important to set high standards for ourselves, striving for perfection or unrealistic ideals can have a detrimental impact on self-love. When we inevitably fall short of our sky-high expectations, we have a tendency to judge and criticize ourselves. It's like we have this little voice in our head that loves to point out every flaw, mistake, or imperfection.

If you find yourself caught up in a cycle of negative self-talk, this spell will help you silence your inner critic and release perfectionism with the support of amazonite and smoky quartz. Amazonite is a stone of truth and hope that encourages self-compassion. It reminds you that it's okay to make mistakes, stumble, and learn along the way. Additionally, smoky quartz is a grounding and detoxifying stone that clears away self-imposed pressures and limiting beliefs. It assists in dissolving self-doubt and replacing it with a sense of inner strength and self-assurance.

Materials:
Amazonite
Smoky quartz
Paper and pen

Directions:
In a comfortable seated position, holding the amazonite and smoky quartz in each hand, close your eyes and feel their energy. Visualize a soothing blue light emanating from the amazonite and a soft white light from the smoky quartz. Connect to their supportive energies and know that you are in a safe space to honor your emotions. After a few minutes, take the paper and pen and write down any negative thoughts or self-critical statements that come to mind. Be honest and allow your thoughts to flow without judgment. Read through each item your list and reflect on its impact on how you perceive yourself. Now, reframe each negative thought as a positive statements of self-love, and write it down. For example, you can reframe "I'm not good enough," as, "I am worthy of and deserving of love and acceptance exactly as I am." Allow the energy of both crystals to infuse these positive statements with kindness and tenderness.

Once you have written down all of the reframed thoughts, hold amazonite over your heart, and smoky quartz over your stomach. Take a deep breath and recite each positive self-love statement aloud, allowing the words to resonate deeply within you. Feel the truth and power behind these statements, repeating them as many times as you feel is necessary to truly internalize the affirmations. When you're done, place the crystals and list of positive affirmations in your bathroom or near a mirror. Recite one of the affirmations aloud whenever you see yourself to reinforce your intentions and practice self-love.

MOTIVATION SPELL JAR

Take inspired action toward your goals with this motivation spell jar. Whether you're looking to start a new business endeavor or establish a healthy habit, this spell will help you tackle your to-do list with confidence and determination.

A spell jar is a magickal tool that combines various ingredients such as herbs, crystals, oils, and symbols, enclosed in a jar or container. Its purpose is to harness and amplify the energy of these elements to manifest specific intentions or desires. The act of creating and working with a spell jar allows you to actively participate in the manifestation process and connect with the energies of the ingredients and symbols used. Feel free to modify this spell jar to your liking, and as always, use your intuition when selecting ingredients.

Materials:
Small glass jar or bottle with a tight lid
Garnet
Tiger's eye
Carnelian
A bay leaf
Pen
A strand of your hair

Directions:
Cleanse and charge the crystals by placing them in the sunlight for a few hours. When you're ready to assemble the jar or bottle, hold the garnet in your hand and say: "Garnet to motivate the body." Visualize yourself experiencing a surge of motivation in your physical body, filling your muscles with strength and vigor. Place the crystal in the bottle. Next, hold the tiger's eye in your hand and say: "Tiger's eye to motivate the mind." Envision your mind being cleared of all distractions and doubts as you embrace a renewed sense of purpose. Place the crystal in the bottle. Hold the carnelian in your hand and say: "Carnelian to motivate the spirit." Imagine a bright orange glow emanating around your entire body, connecting you to your creative and sensual side and renewing your zest for life. Place the crystal in the bottle. Write your specific motivation-related intention or affirmation on the bay leaf, such as, "I am motivated, focused, and driven to achieve my goals." Add it to the jar. Lastly, take a single strand of your hair and place it in the jar.

Seal the jar tightly and hold it in your hands. Envision yourself filled with motivation, determination, and commitment. Feel the powerful energy of the crystals and the intention you've set. Place the jar in a location where you'll see it often. Whenever you need a boost of motivation, gently shake the jar to activate the ingredients and hold it in your hands for a few minutes to reconnect with your intention. To start your day off with a burst of energy, meditate with the jar to shake off lethargy and stay committed to your goals.

INNER CHILD HEALING RITUAL

Inner child work involves creating a safe, compassionate space to acknowledge and heal any emotional wounds, trauma, or unmet needs from childhood. It recognizes that our experiences during early development can significantly impact how we behave as adults, as well as our ability to love ourselves. Through inner child healing, we are able to reconnect with the wounded or neglected parts of ourselves and gain insight into how our past experiences shape our present reality. This process allows us to release limiting beliefs and provide ourselves the love, care, and nurturing that our younger self may have missed.

This ritual is designed to help you begin a gentle conversation with your inner child. Listen attentively and respond with kindness and reassurance. It's important to note that inner child work can be a deeply personal and sensitive process, so if you feel overwhelmed or if past traumas resurface, it's essential to seek support from a qualified mental health professional or a therapist.

Materials:
Comforting items such as stuffed animals, favorite childhood toys, or photographs
Black tourmaline
Carnelian
Rose quartz
Paper and pen

Directions:

Gather objects that symbolize nurturing, playfulness, and comfort to represent your inner child and arrange them in front of you. Come to a seated position and hold the black tourmaline in your hands. Take a few deep breaths, centering yourself in the present moment. Visualize its protective energy surrounding you like a shield. Imagine any negative energy being absorbed by the crystal, leaving you feeling safe and secure.

Close your eyes and visualize your inner child standing before you. Take a moment to greet your younger self with love and acceptance, letting them know you are here to provide support and healing. Place the carnelian crystal on your lower abdomen. This crystal symbolizes creativity, passion, and joy. Visualize its warm and vibrant energy flowing into your inner child, igniting their sense of playfulness and curiosity. Now hold the rose quartz crystal over your heart center, allowing its gentle and loving energy to permeate your being. Feel the unconditional love and compassion radiating from the crystal, nurturing your inner child's needs.

Now begin a dialogue with your inner child. Ask them how they're feeling, what they need, or if there's anything they want to share with you. Listen without judgment, then write down a few positive affirmations specifically tailored for your inner child's healing. These affirmations should emphasize self-love and self-acceptance, such as, "I deserve happiness and love in my life," or, "I am re-parenting myself with compassion and understanding." Hold the paper with your affirmations close to your heart and read each one aloud. Feel the power of these words resonating within you and visualize a gentle light surrounding your inner child. Imagine this light dissolving any remaining pain or wounds, transforming them into love and healing as your inner child merges with your present self. Sit in silence for a few minutes as you feel the integration and renewed sense of wholeness within you.

HONEY BATH ATTRACTION SPELL

When life needs a little more sweetness, just add honey. The use of honey can be traced back to ancient times, where honey was considered a sacred food with healing properties. The sweetness of honey was thought to attract the sweetness of life, and its viscosity was believed to be a symbol of abundance. Today, honey is still used in magickal and spiritual practices to promote feelings of harmony, kindness, joy, love, and happiness.

By infusing your bathwater with honey, you'll be able to invite new blessings, positive experiences, and opportunities into your life. The spell also acts as a catalyst for deepening the sweetness and connection in your relationships, whether they are platonic, romantic, or familial.

Materials:
Matches or lighter
Pink or red candles
Small bowl
2 tbsp of honey (preferably raw or organic)
A handful of fresh or dried rose petals or few
  drops of rose essential oil
Rose quartz

Directions:
Set the mood by dimming the lights in your bathroom to create a serene atmosphere. Light the pink or red candles and place them around the bathtub to inspire passion and harmony. In a small bowl, mix the honey with a handful of fresh or dried rose petals, or a few drops of rose essential oil. As you stir the mixture, focus on imbuing it with the energy of love, beauty, and attraction. Visualize the honey as a magickal essence that will enhance your allure and draw love into your life.

Draw a bath with warm water, then slowly pour the infused honey into the tub, stirring clockwise as you chant, "As I soak in golden comb, let sweetness flow into my home." Before you step into the tub, hold the rose quartz crystal in your hands and think about what you'd like to call into your life. Be specific and envision it clearly in your mind, then step into the bath. Submerge yourself in the honey-infused water, allowing your body to soak in the energy of attraction and love. If you wash yourself, start at your feet then move up to your head, as this will draw blessings toward you instead of flushing them away. Once you're done, exit the tub and let yourself drip-dry. This allows the magickal effects of the bath to seep into your skin and aura. Extinguish the candles and drain the tub, visualizing any negative energy being carried away with the bathwater.

SPEAK YOUR TRUTH SPELL

Have you ever questioned the validity or worthiness of your own thoughts and feelings, or have held back from saying what you really felt because you were afraid of how it would be received? We all have those moments of uncertainty and self-doubt, wondering if what we say really matters. While it can be difficult to speak our truth, it's important to let our voice be heard, because when we courageously share our thoughts and express our needs, we are able to validate our own experiences and establish healthy boundaries which are essential for self-love. This process also allows us to become more self-assured and make decisions that align with our authentic desires.

In this spell, you'll learn how to tap in to your innermost truth with the power of blue sodalite. Blue sodalite resonates with the throat chakra, enhancing communication and mental clarity. This stone represents honesty, logic, and balance, bringing integrity to your emotions and increasing self-awareness.

Materials:
Blue sodalite
Paper and pen

Directions:
Find a quiet and comfortable space where you can focus. Hold the blue sodalite over your throat and close your eyes. Harness its calming energy and take three deep breaths, allowing yourself to connect with your inner thoughts and emotions. Then reflect on an area or situation in your life where you feel like your voice isn't being heard, and write it down. For instance, "When my team at work discusses new ideas, my suggestions are ignored." Next, take another three breaths to ground yourself in the present.

Now, transform your statement into a positive affirmation. With a fresh perspective and on a new piece of paper, rewrite the situation to infuse it with positivity. For example, the original statement could be reframed as, "My ideas are valued and embraced, and we collaborate on creating new products." With confidence and intention, speak the positive rewrite three times. Allow the words to flow from your lips and into the universe, symbolizing your commitment to assertively express your needs and desires. Hang onto the rewrite as a positive reminder of your new perspective and dispose of the original statement to part ways with old beliefs.

As you conclude the spell, remember that the power lies within you to bring about change. Whenever you find yourself in one of those negative situations, recall the positive rewrite associated with it. Let your inner voice guide you to speak up and assert yourself, confidently expressing your desires and opinions. Trust that by speaking your truth, you are creating a reality where your voice is heard and respected.

LOVE LETTERS TO THE SELF

It's time to be your own secret admirer. In this ritual, you will embark on a heartfelt journey of reflection, appreciation, and healing by writing love letters to your past, present, and future self. The process of committing your thoughts and emotions to paper can be powerful, and these letters provide a space to acknowledge your experiences, celebrate your triumphs, and offer words of encouragement and support to the different versions of who you are.

As you begin to write these letters, remember to approach the practice with an open heart, vulnerability, and kindness. See yourself through a lens of compassion and give thanks for every stage of your personal evolution.

Materials:
Rose quartz
Pen
3 sheets of paper
Amethyst
Clear quartz

Directions:
Hold the rose quartz crystal in your hand and set an intention to cultivate self-love, allowing its soothing and supportive energy to fill you up. Set the crystal down, and address each piece of paper with "Dearest (Your Name)," and write a love letter to your past self on the first sheet, your present self on the second, and your future self on the third. Hold the amethyst in your other hand. Allow its calming energy to flow into your words, bringing clarity and a deeper understanding of yourself.

On the past sheet, express love, compassion, and forgiveness to the person you used to be. Acknowledge any challenges you have overcome and emphasize the lessons learned.

On the present sheet, embrace and appreciate who you are now. Celebrate your accomplishments, unique qualities, and inner beauty. Express gratitude for the journey that has led you to this point.

On the future sheet, show love and anticipation for who you are becoming. Encourage and support them, envisioning a life of love, joy, and fulfillment. Embrace the possibilities and express excitement for continued growth.

Once completed, place the clear quartz on top of the love letters, amplifying their intentions and energies. Hold the rose quartz in your hand again and speak affirmations of self-love such as, "I love and honor all aspects of myself," or; "I am worthy of love and joy in all phases of my life." Keep the love letters and crystals in a safe and sacred place, such as a special box or dedicated self-love altar. Return to them whenever you need a reminder of your own worth and how far you have come.

MANIFESTATION SPELL BOX

Bring your deepest desires to life with this manifestation spell box. A spell box is a container filled with items, symbols, and intentions that are carefully combined to create a focused energy for a specific purpose or outcome.

Spell boxes can be used for various purposes, including manifestation. It's about bringing something you want or envision into your life, whether that be a new job opportunity or a romantic relationship.

While you can customize the items in your spell box to align with any intention, I recommend using crystals like citrine, clear quartz, green aventurine, pyrite, tiger's eye, and jade, as they are known for their manifestation-boosting abilities.

Materials:

Clear quartz
Paper and pen
Box or container
 with a lid
Citrine

Green aventurine
Items that align with
 your intention or
 have a personal
 significance to you

Directions:

Hold the clear quartz in your hand and close your eyes. Think about what you want to manifest in your life. Once you've clearly defined your intention, write it down on a piece of paper. Place the clear quartz, citrine, and green aventurine inside the small box along with your written intention. As you place each crystal in the box, visualize it infusing your intention with abundance, strength, and good fortune. Draw a compass on a piece of paper and add it to the box—this will help whatever you seek find its way to you. Place additional items in the box that align with your intention or have a personal significance to you. For instance, if you wish to manifest financial abundance, you might place some cash or a small pouch of coins in the box.

Once the box is filled, hold it in your hands and state your intention aloud. For example, "I am a powerful creator, manifesting my desires with ease," or, "My dreams and intentions manifest effortlessly and in perfect timing." Speak from your heart, infusing your words with belief and passion. Close the box and hold it in your hands one final time. Visualize a protective shield forming around it, sealing the energy within. Trust that the universe is working in your favor to bring your desires into reality. Find a special place for your manifestation spell box, such as your altar or sacred space. You can choose to keep it visible or in a private location. Continue to regularly spend time near the box, focusing your thoughts on what you want to manifest, and thinking about the ways to take inspired action toward your goals.

DIVINE INSIGHTS SCRYING RITUAL

If you start to feel lost or confused on your self-love journey, this scrying ritual will help you find the answers you seek within. Scrying is an ancient divination practice that involves using a reflective or illuminated surface such as a crystal, mirror, or water to enter a trance-like state. Images and symbols may appear on the object's surface, which are later interpreted to reveal hidden truths. The purpose of scrying is to gain insight, clarity, and guidance by tapping into the subconscious mind and the depths of one's intuition.

A black obsidian mirror or crystal ball is ideal for scrying, but if one is not available to you, don't worry—you can use a dark-colored bowl and water instead. I recommend waiting until nightfall to perform this ritual, as scrying is traditionally associated with moonlight. However, if you'd like to try it during the day, turn off all the lights to make your room as dark as possible.

Materials:
Dark-colored bowl
Water
Matches or lighter
Candle (any colour)
Obsidian
Silver coin

Directions:
Set up your scrying area by placing the dark-colored bowl in front of you and filling it with water. Light the candle and place it next to the bowl. Hold the obsidian crystal in your hands and take a few deep breaths to relax your body. Release any tension or distractions, allowing yourself to be fully present. Think about a specific question you'd like to ask. Once it's clear in your mind, gently set the obsidian down in front of the bowl.

Take the silver coin and hold it in your hand (the coin will serve as a focal point during the ritual). As you hold it, infuse it with your intentions for clarity and insight. Drop the silver coin into the water-filled bowl, allowing it to create ripples. Gaze at the ripples as they expand outward, keeping your question at the forefront of your mind. When the water becomes still, shift your eyes to the coin. Allow your mind to enter a calm and receptive state. Let your vision go blurry as you maintain a soft and unfocused gaze. You might notice the surface of the water becoming murky, misty, or cloudy, allowing images or visions to appear. Watch for letters, words, shapes, symbols, or entire scenes to emerge and make a mental note of them, along with any thoughts or emotions that surface during the session. I recommend gazing for no longer than fifteen minutes, though you can adapt the length to your preference and intuition. Once the water has become clear again, snuff out the candle and remove the coin from the bowl. Take a moment to reflect on what you saw, noting any significant revelations and insights.

ULTIMATE RICHES AFFIRMATION JAR

Welcome abundance into your life by creating an affirmation jar. An affirmation jar is a simple yet powerful tool that can be used to support positive thinking and manifestation. It involves writing down statements that affirm the reality you desire to create in your life, placing them in a jar, and regularly engaging with them to reinforce positive beliefs and intentions.

Materials:
Small glass jar with a lid
Green aventurine (or any other green or gold colored crystal)
Small slips of paper and pen
Green ribbon or string

You can create an affirmation jar for any intention you desire, but this one is specifically geared toward cultivating prosperity, both internally and externally. I recommend using crystals with abundance-boosting properties, such as green aventurine, jade, pyrite, or citrine for best results.

Directions:

Hold the green aventurine crystal in your hands and visualize it being cleansed and energized by a pure, vibrant, white light. Come to a comfortable seated position and set the stone aside. Reflect on your desires for abundance in your life. What does abundance mean to you? It could be financial prosperity, opportunities, joy, love, or any form of abundance that resonates with you. Allow these intentions to fill your mind and heart.

Take the slips of paper and write down your affirmations. Be positive and specific. These could be statements for attracting abundance, such as, "I am open to receiving new career opportunities. I am a beacon of good fortune." Or, ones for recognizing your inner worth, such as, "I am proud of myself. I trust in my abilities." Write down as many affirmations as you'd like, making each one meaningful to you.

Pick up your crystal and hold it in your hands. Visualize prosperous energies flowing into the stone, infusing it with your intentions and becoming a magnet for abundance. Place the crystal inside the glass jar. Then, fold each slip of paper with your affirmations and add them to the jar, one by one. With each slip, imagine your intentions being stored within the crystal and sealed by the jar. Close the lid of the jar and hold it in your hands. Express gratitude for the abundance that is already present in your life and for the abundance that is yet to come. Feel a deep sense of appreciation and trust in the universe's ability to manifest abundance for you.

Take the green ribbon or string and tie it around the neck of the jar, creating a decorative bow. This adds an extra touch of energy and symbolism, representing the flow and growth of abundance. Find a special place for your jar where you'll be able to see it regularly, such as your desk, altar, or bedside table. Whenever you pass by or feel called to do so, take a moment to hold the jar and visualize your affirmations coming to life.

SOUL SOOTHER ROOM MIST RITUAL

Inner peace is just one spritz away. This magickal room mist uses the calming properties of amethyst and lavender to melt away stress and promote relaxation. Use it to unwind after a long day of work or put a stop to anxious or scattered thoughts before bed.

A room mist, or sacred spray, is a blend of water, essential oils, and other natural ingredients that can be used to infuse a space with specific energies or intentions. It is commonly used in spiritual or magickal practices to cleanse, purify, and bless a room. Room mists can enhance rituals by creating a sacred atmosphere. They help to set the mood and shift the energy of the space, making it more conducive to meditation or spell work.

Materials:
Amethyst
2 fl oz (60 ml) of distilled water
1 tsp of witch hazel
8 drops of lavender essential oil
Dried lavender sprigs or buds (optional)
A small misting bottle

Directions:
Rinse the amethyst under running water to remove any physical or energetic residue from the stone. Hold the crystal in your hands and close your eyes. Connect to its calming and soothing energy as you feel its tranquil vibrations permeating your being. Combine the distilled water, witch hazel, lavender essential oil, and amethyst in the misting bottle. If desired, add dried lavender sprigs or buds. Close the bottle tightly and shake it gently, blending the ingredients together. As you shake, envision a peaceful purple glow emanating from the bottle, radiating with serenity. Take a moment to hold the bottle in your hands, feeling its energy and the intentions you've infused into the mist. You may choose to say a simple affirmation or blessing at this time, such as, "I let go of stress and embrace inner peace."

Find a room in your home that you wish to infuse with calming energy. Stand in the center of the room and spritz the mist into the air, allowing it to settle and fill the space. As you spray, visualize the purple glow from the bottle spreading throughout the room, enveloping it in a soothing aura and creating a serene sanctuary. Take a moment to inhale the scent, allowing its calming properties to wash over you. Store the mist in a cool, dark place. Before each subsequent use, give the bottle a gentle shake to activate the ingredients and intentions. Repeat the ritual as needed to refresh the energy of your space, or whenever you desire a moment of tranquility. Your spray should keep for two to four months.

GARDEN OF GRATITUDE RITUAL

Gratitude, like a nourishing soil, provides the fertile ground upon which self-love can grow and flourish. It is a profound acknowledgement and appreciation of the blessings, abundance, and beauty that surrounds us. By cultivating gratitude, we create a rich garden within our hearts where self-love can take root and bloom.

Whether you're struggling with negativity or a pessimistic outlook, or simply want to be more present, creating a gratitude altar can serve as a powerful tool to shift your perspective. Gratitude helps to alleviate stress, anxiety, and feelings of unworthiness by focusing our attention on the blessings we have in our lives. By recognizing even the smallest joys and gifts, we are able to cultivate a positive mindset that supports self-love.

Materials:
Matches or lighter
Incense or essential oils
Green or gold cloth
Crystals that represent abundance
  (such as jade, citrine, or pyrite)
Symbols of things you're grateful for
  (such as photos of loved ones)
Bowl of fruit (such as apples or grapes)
Green or gold candle

Directions:
Find a quiet and sacred space, such as a table, shelf, or other surface. Cleanse the space by lighting some incense or using essential oils in an essential oil diffuser to circulate their aroma. Place down a green or gold cloth as the base. Intuitively arrange the crystals on the cloth to your liking, choosing ones that represent abundance, such as jade and citrine. Now add in items that symbolize things that you're grateful for, such as your health or career. These can be small objects that represent achievements, hobbies, or experiences that have brought you joy. Place them with intention, acknowledging the blessings they represent.

Incorporate photos of loved ones or moments that hold special significance. Arrange them in a way that feels meaningful and give thanks for the love and connection they bring to your life. Add a bowl or basket of fruit symbolizing abundance and the bounty of the season. Express gratitude for the nourishment they provide. You can choose a variety of fruits or ones that hold personal meaning.

Place the green or gold candle in the middle of the altar and light it. Set an intention for gratitude, such as, "I am grateful for the gift of life and all the experiences it brings."

Take a few moments to stand or sit in front of your gratitude altar. Breathe deeply, grounding yourself in the present moment. Spend a few moments in meditation, allowing gratitude to fill your being. Visualize this gratitude expanding from your heart and radiating out into the universe, attracting even more blessings into your life. Whenever you feel the need, return to your gratitude altar to give thanks and uplift your spirit.

EMOTIONAL HEALING SPELL JAR

When we think about health, we often focus on our physical body, but tending to our emotional body is just as important. Our emotional body is a reflection of our thoughts, feelings, and inner world. When we experience emotional distress, it can not only manifest as physical symptoms (such as headaches, muscle tension, and digestive issues), but negatively impact our mental health too.

If you've been struggling with hurt, sadness, or pain, this nurturing spell jar can serve as a powerful catalyst for healing. Filled with supportive crystals and soothing herbs and flowers, it transforms feelings of despair and heartache into vibrations of peace, hope, and wisdom. I highly recommend this spell jar for anyone who is experiencing loss or grief or those who are recovering from a breakup.

Materials:
Rose quartz
Amethyst
Clear quartz
Small glass jar or bottle with a tight lid
A handful of dried chamomile
Lavender essential oil
Small piece of paper and pen
Band-aid or gauze

Directions:
Cleanse your crystals by rinsing them under running water or placing them in the moonlight for a few hours. Gather a small glass jar or bottle. Place the rose quartz, amethyst, and clear quartz inside the jar, one at a time. As you add each crystal, visualize their healing energy enveloping you, soothing any emotional pain or turmoil. Next, add a handful of dried chamomile, along with a few drops of lavender essential oil. Take a few deep breaths to calm your mind and body.

Take the small piece of paper and write down any specific emotions or experiences you wish to heal from. Pour your heart into these words, expressing your desire for emotional healing and release. Know that this is a safe space to open your heart and allow yourself to feel. Open the band-aid and stick it to the back of the paper. If you have gauze, attach it to the paper with tape. Fold the paper and place it inside the bottle, allowing the crystals and herbs to infuse your intention with tenderness and compassion.

Hold the jar in your hands and speak the following affirmation aloud: "I am whole, I am healed, I am at peace." Seal the jar tightly and place it in a safe and sacred space where you can see it regularly, such as your bedroom or a meditation area. Whenever you feel down, take a moment to hold the jar and connect with its healing energy.

RENEWAL SHOWER RITUAL

Purify your aura and revitalize your spirit with this renewal shower ritual. This ritual is designed to awaken the senses and wash away the energetic and emotional blockages that are hindering your capacity to fully experience and embrace self-love, such as negative self-talk, unresolved emotions, and limiting beliefs.

Like a ritual bath, the process of showering can become a powerful and effective way to engage in energetic cleansing when done with intention and mindfulness. This ritual uses water, a symbol of purification and renewal, along with various healing herbs to gently dislodge and remove energetic debris.

Eucalyptus, roses, basil, thyme, peppermint, lavender, and sage are all great options, but use whatever resonates with you. If fresh herbs are not available to you, you can always use the essential oils of herbs and put a few drops by your feet for a similar effect.

Materials:
Fresh or dried herbs and flowers
Clear quartz
String or rubber band

Directions:
Gather your favorite fragrant herbs and/or flowers. Bundle them together tightly with a string or rubber band. The bundle should be approximately 1–2 inches in diameter. Tie a string around the end of the bundle and hang it around the shower head, then plug the drain.

Set your intention for renewal and transformation by meditating with clear quartz. Hold the crystal in your hand and connect to its cleansing and renewing properties as you repeat the following: "As I step into the sacred waters of cleansing, I release all that weighs me down." Turn on the water and once it's warm enough, step into the shower. Place the clear quartz in the tub, allowing it to infuse the water with its healing energy (being mindful not to step on it). Close your eyes and let the warm water envelop you. As you shower, feel its purifying properties gently cleanse not only your physical body, but also your energy field. Let it carry away any residual stress and worries. Surrender to the sensations and let go of anything that no longer serves you.

Take deep breaths, inhaling the invigorating aroma of the herbs. The steam from the warm water will release the fragrant properties of the herbs, creating a magickal and rejuvenating atmosphere. While the water continues to flow, recite affirmations or positive statements that resonate with renewal, such as, "My spirit is light. I am reborn." When you are ready to conclude the ritual, remove the clear quartz and any herbs that have fallen, then unplug the drain. Let the water carry away any negative energy, allowing it to be transformed and released.

SERENITY CRYSTAL GRID

Bring a sense of calm and peace to your home and life with this serenity crystal grid. Featuring a combination of soothing and harmonizing stones, this grid is a powerful tool for promoting tranquility and relaxation. It is especially useful for anyone dealing with chaotic or disruptive situations or those who simply want to tune in to their inner zen.

Crystal grids come in a variety of shapes, each of which carry a different energy. This one uses a double circle formation. Circular shaped grids represent harmony and balance as they distribute energy evenly in all directions. They also symbolize wholeness, belonging, and positive emotions, guiding one toward a state of peace, self-acceptance, and self-love.

Materials:
A flat surface to create your grid (table or cloth)
Match and lighters
Incense
1 large moonstone
3 medium amazonite
3 medium rose quartz
6 small blue lace agate
6 small clear quartz

Directions:
Cleanse your sacred space and crystals by lighting some incense and wafting it around the room and stones. Set up the grid on a flat surface such as a table, or lay down a cloth to use as a base. Place the large moonstone in the center of your grid. This stone symbolizes serenity and acts as a focal point for the grid. Around the moonstone, arrange the three medium sized amazonite crystals in an inner ring. These crystals are known for their calming and spiritually uplifting properties. In the same inner ring, place the three medium rose quartz crystals so that they alternate with the amazonite. These stones promote self-love, compassion, and emotional healing. Next, create an outer ring. Place the six small blue lace agate stones in this ring. Their soothing and tranquil energy helps to calm the mind and reduce anxiety. Finally, complete the outer ring with the six small clear quartz stones. These amplify the energies of the other crystals and help remove stagnant or negative energy.

Take a moment to set your intention for the grid. Focus on cultivating serenity and inner peace in your life. You can silently or verbally affirm your intention, expressing your desire for tranquility, emotional balance, and relaxation. For example, "I am at peace with myself and the world around me." Once the grid is set up, you can spend time near it meditating, journaling, or simply being present. Allow the energies of the crystals to surround you and fill you as you embrace stillness and find solace within. Let this grid serve as a reminder of your power to cultivate inner peace at any time, even amidst life's challenges.

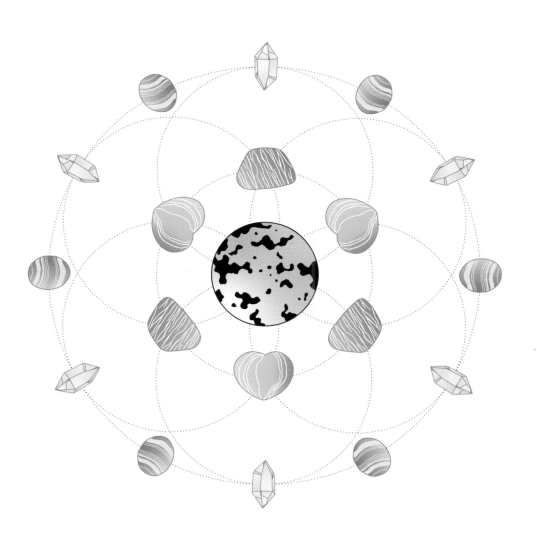

ROSE FACE MASK RITUAL

Harness the healing power of roses and pamper your skin with a luxurious DIY face mask. This face mask is infused with crushed rose petals to promote self-love as well as inner and outer beauty. Roses have been used for centuries in beauty rituals due to their soothing, moisturizing, and rejuvenating properties. Their petals are rich in vitamins and antioxidants, providing deep hydration to the skin while reducing redness and inflammation.

Rose is generally considered safe for all skin types, even sensitive or irritated skin, as it is known for its gentle and calming effect. However, make sure the roses you use are certified organic or from an unsprayed plant, as florist or commercial roses are heavily treated with pesticides, which you don't want to apply to your skin. If you're new to using rose-infused products on your face, patch test a small area to check for allergic reactions or irritations before applying the mask to your entire face.

Materials:
2 tbsp of organic rose petals
Mortar and pestle (or food processor)
1 tbsp of organic honey
2 tbsp of plain yogurt
Small bowl
Spoon
1–2 tsp of water or rose water
Rose quartz
Your favorite toner, serum, and moisturizer

Directions:
Take the organic rose petals and place them in the mortar and pestle or food processor. Gently grind the petals using a circular motion until they form a fine powder. If you don't have a mortar and pestle, you can use a food processor to achieve the same result. Transfer the ground rose petals to a clean bowl. Add the organic honey and plain yogurt to the bowl and stir with a spoon to combine. Slowly mix in small amounts of water or rose water until a smooth, even paste forms. Use less water for a thicker consistency, or more for a thinner mask.

Take the rose quartz crystal and hold it in your hands over the bowl. Close your eyes and set your intention for the face mask by repeating the following aloud: "Let roses red and honey sweet, fill my heart with love complete." Visualize the rose quartz infusing the mask with love, compassion, and positive energy, enhancing its properties. Set the crystal to the side and apply the rose face mask mixture evenly to your face, avoiding the eye area. Once the mask is applied, take a moment to relax and let the ingredients work their magick. You can lie down, play soothing music, or think about all the things that you love in your life and express gratitude for them. Allow the mask to sit on your face for 15–20 minutes, then rinse it off with cool water. Pat your skin dry with a clean towel and spend a few minutes admiring your rejuvenated skin in the mirror. Proceed with your regular skincare routine by applying your usual toners, serums, and moisturizers.

MOON MILK BATH RITUAL

When you need a little TLC, turn to this moon milk bath to soothe the senses and honor your emotions. A milk bath is a warm bath of water that you pour milk into. The milk can be liquid or powdered, and animal or plant-based. The benefits of the milk vary depending on its source. Animal milk contains proteins and fats that moisturize the skin. When buying animal milk, try to stick with ethically sourced and eco-friendly brands, or opt for dairy-free alternatives. In terms of plant-based milk, oat milk and coconut milk are great options. Oats have been shown to decrease inflammation and irritation, and the rich fats in coconut milk offer ample hydration.

I recommend performing this ritual at night to connect with lunar energy, as the moon represents emotions, intuition, and the subconscious—making it easier for you tap in to hidden feelings.

Materials:

Matches or lighter (optional)
Candles (optional)
Soft music or nature sounds (optional)
4 cups (960 ml) of milk
5 drops of lavender essential oil
5 drops of jasmine essential oil
2 tbsp of bath oil (such as coconut, olive, or jojoba)
Fresh or dried lavender or rose petals (optional)
1 cup (240 g) of Epsom salts
Moonstone
A handful of fresh or dried flowers (optional)

Directions:

Create a peaceful ambiance in your bathing area. Dim the lights, light candles, or play soft music or nature sounds if desired. Fill up your tub with warm water, then add in the milk of your choosing, lavender and jasmine essential oils, bath oil, and Epsom salts. If desired, scatter fresh or dried flowers, such as lavender or rose petals, on the surface of the bathwater.

Meditate with the moonstone crystal in hand before you enter the tub. As you hold the stone, allow its comforting and calming properties to bring you to a place of openness, receptivity, and stillness. Breathe deeply and on the exhale, state something that you'd like to release out loud. For example, you could say something such as, "I release all frustration." Set the moonstone away from the tub, as water can damage moonstone, then carefully step into the bath. Let the warm water cleanse your mind of negative thoughts and worries. Take your time to relax and soak in the healing energy of the bath. Close your eyes, visualize the moon's gentle glow, and let go of any stress or tension. When you're ready to exit the bath, rinse your body with fresh water to remove any excess milk, then pat yourself dry with a clean towel (be careful as you stand up and exit the tub, as the milk can make the tub extra slippery). If any uncomfortable emotions or memories surfaced during the bath, spend a few minutes journaling in the moonlight about them to explore your feelings and uncover intuitive insights. Place the moonstone under your pillow or by your nightstand to promote deep sleep.

CHAKRA HEALING TEA RITUAL

Dissolve energetic blockages and promote total chakra healing with this sacred tea ritual. The act of preparing and consuming tea in a mindful manner encourages us to slow down, be present, and engage our senses fully. In this ritual, we will explore the delicate interplay between the mind, body, and spirit, using tea as a vessel for intention and healing, and crystals for energetic support.

The chakras, or the body's energy centers, play a vital role in our overall wellbeing. Each chakra is associated with specific qualities and influences different aspects of our physical, emotional, and spiritual selves. When a chakra is blocked or imbalanced, it can lead to issues and create a sense of internal conflict that causes discomfort. However, through this tea ritual, we can bring healing to these energy centers and cultivate harmony within.

Materials:
4 cups (960 ml) of purified water
Your favorite loose-leaf tea or tea bag
Tea cup or mug
Tea strainer (if using loose-leaf tea)
7 crystals (one that corresponds with each
  chakra. See chapter 2)

Directions:
Bring 4 cups of fresh, purified water to a roiling boil, then pour into a tea cup or mug over your favorite loose leaf-tea or tea bag. Set the filled tea cup or mug in front of you. As the tea steeps, take a moment to hold each crystal corresponding to the chakras, one by one. Close your eyes and connect with the energy of each stone, visualizing it radiating with the specific color and qualities associated with that chakra. Start with the root chakra crystal and place it near the cup. State your intention to balance and align your root chakra for stability and grounding. Repeat this process with each crystal, placing them in a circle around the tea cup in the following chakra order: sacral, solar plexus, heart, throat, third eye, and crown. Once all the crystals are arranged, let the tea cool for a few minutes. During this time, visualize a beam of light flowing from each crystal into the tea. Imagine each beam is a different color that matches its associated chakra, creating a rainbow effect. Envision the energy from the crystals blending with the tea, forming a potent elixir for chakra healing.

After the tea has cooled, remove the loose-leaf tea or tea bag. Hold the cup in your hands and focus on your intention for opening and aligning the chakras. Begin to slowly drink the tea. Take a sip, pause and feel the warmth of the tea radiating to your root chakra, near the base of your spine. Repeat this process until you've worked your way through all seven chakras in their proper order. You can continue this cycle until you've finished the tea, or simply enjoy the remainder of your drink.

BALANCE SPELL

Finding balance in life can be tricky, but it's an essential ingredient for self-love. The concept of balance encompasses different dimensions of our being. It involves creating an equilibrium between work and play, solitude and socializing, and giving and receiving. If we tip the scales too far in one direction while neglecting others, it can take a physical and mental toll and lead to burnout and exhaustion. Balance helps us prioritize our needs and establish healthy boundaries so that we can foster a sustainable and nourishing lifestyle.

If you're having trouble juggling multiple responsibilities and roles, use this spell to bring your life back into balance and foster a harmonious rhythm in your day-to-day. While this spell features clear quartz and black tourmaline, feel free to use any combination of white, clear, and black stones. You can also use two pieces of amethyst or fluorite.

Materials:
White candle
Black candle
Matches or lighter
Clear quartz
Black tourmaline
2 pieces of paper
Pen
Fireproof bowl or dish

Directions:
Find a quiet and clean space to perform the spell. Arrange the white and black candles in front of you, side-by-side. Place the white candle on the left, symbolizing light, and the black candle on the right, representing darkness. Light the candles and come to a comfortable seated position to meditate. Hold clear quartz in your left hand and black tourmaline in your right hand, then close your eyes. Take a few deep breaths, slowing down each inhale and exhale until you feel completely centered.

Take one piece of paper and write down the things you wish to have more of in your life. On the other sheet of paper, write down the things you would like decrease or release.

With care, hold the paper with your intentions for what you want more of to the flame of the white candle, and the paper for what you wish to release to the flame of the black candle. As they burn simultaneously, repeat the following incantation aloud: "As yin is to yang, as dark is to light, may I cultivate balance in all aspects of life." Transfer the lit pieces of paper to a fireproof bowl or dish to continue burning as you repeat the incantation. Once the papers are done burning, let the candles burn out.

Note: never leave a lit candle unattended. If you can't wait for the candles to burn down, extinguish them with a candle snuffer, or you can smother the flame by placing a non-flammable lid on top of the jar.

HEART OPENING MEDITATION

Unlock the power of your heart with this healing meditation. In this fast-paced and often hectic world, it is easy to become disconnected from our hearts and the wellspring of love and compassion that resides in its depths. When our heart chakra is blocked or imbalanced, we may struggle to connect with our emotions, experience a lack of empathy, or have difficulty giving and receiving love. We might hold onto past hurts, harbor resentments, or find it challenging to forgive. This can lead to feelings of loneliness and emotional distress.

Fortunately, there are a number of practices that can help to restore balance and flow to the heart chakra, such as this heart opening meditation. In this meditation, you'll learn how to consciously open your heart space and invite in feelings of love and inner peace. By becoming aware of any barriers or blockages that may be present, you'll be able to acknowledge and release yourself from the burden of past hurts and create space for healing and growth.

Materials:
Rose quartz or your favorite heart chakra stone

Directions:
Find a comfortable and quiet space where you can relax and immerse yourself in this mediation. Sit down, close your eyes, and take a few slow breaths, allowing your body to relax and your mind to quiet. Now, rub your palms together, creating a gentle warmth and energizing sensation. Place one hand over your heart and the other hand on your belly. Breathe deeply and bring your awareness to your heart center, located in the center of your chest. Visualize a soft, green light glowing in this space, emanating with love. Allow this light to grow brighter with each breath you take.

As you continue to breathe, imagine love flowing in and out of your heart, like a beautiful radiant light. As you inhale, feel this loving energy filling your heart space, and as you exhale, envision it radiating outward, touching every aspect of your being and extending out into the world. After a few minutes, your entire body should be enveloped in a green glow. Once your heart feels full, take the rose quartz or your favorite heart chakra stone in your hands and hold it over your chest and speak an affirmation for love out loud, such as, "My heart is open, and I am worthy of love," or, "Unconditional love flows freely from my heart." Allow the affirmation to resonate within you, reinforcing your intention to open your heart and invite love and compassion into your life. Carry the energy of this meditation with you throughout your day and keep your crystal nearby as a reminder of the limitless love that flows within and through you.

GAIA GROUNDING RITUAL

Grounding is a powerful practice that supports our self-love journey by fostering stability and balance within ourselves. It involves creating a strong connection with the earth's energy through physical contact, visualization techniques, or meditation. In the midst of life's whirlwind, grounding offers a sanctuary of stillness and an opportunity to invoke mindfulness in our day-to-day. When we engage in this practice, we are not only able to root ourselves in the present and better attune to our physical bodies, but stay grounded in our own truth, values, and self-worth.

To maximize the effects of this ritual, perform the ritual outside and barefoot to allow for a direct connection between your feet and the earth. Spending additional time in nature either before or after the ritual can also enhance its grounding effects.

Materials:
Black tourmaline

Directions:
Find a space where you can comfortably be barefoot, preferably outside, with no sharp objects or hazards. Either stand tall or sit down, with the soles of your feet in contact with the ground. Take a few deep breaths to center yourself and shift your focus to the present moment. Hold the black tourmaline crystal in your hands and feel its strong and stable presence, connecting you to grounding energy.

Close your eyes and concentrate on your breathing, inhaling through your nose and exhaling through your mouth. Allow your breath to become slow, smooth, and steady. Turn your attention to the soles of your feet. Feel your bare feet connecting with the surface beneath you. Imagine roots extending from the soles of your feet, reaching deep into the earth. Visualize these roots intertwining with the earth's energy, anchoring you to the ground. Feel the support and stability of the earth rising up through the roots and into your body.

Place the black tourmaline on the ground in front of you, within your line of sight. Focus on the stone and imagine drawing up the earth's grounding energy through the soles of your feet, up into your body, all the way to the crown of your head. Feel this energy flowing through you, anchoring your entire being. As you exhale, release any tension or stress, allowing it to flow down and dissipate into the earth. Spend a few minutes observing the sensations in your body. Express gratitude for the earth and the solid foundation it provides and slowly open your eyes, maintaining a sense of calm and centeredness. Conclude the ritual by placing the black tourmaline in your pocket or holding it in your hand throughout the day.

ENCYCLOPEDIA OF CRYSTALS

 Amazonite—to enhance communication and self-expression; to promote emotional healing and serenity

 Amethyst—to enhance spiritual growth and intuition; to support inner peace and dreams

 Black tourmaline—to provide protection against negative energy; to promote grounding and stability

 Blue sodalite—to enhance intuition and mental clarity; to promote authentic self-expression

 Carnelian—to ignite passion and creativity; to boost motivation and vitality

 Citrine—to attract abundance and manifest success; to boost self-confidence and motivation

 Clear quartz—to amplify energy and intentions; to enhance clarity and focus

 Garnet—to ignite passion and energize the body; to promote grounding and stability

 Green aventurine—to attract luck and prosperity; to support personal growth

 Green jade—to attract abundance and harmony, to promote emotional balance and self-sufficiency

Hematite—to provide grounding and protection; to promote strength, courage, and resilience

Obsidian—to shield against negativity and provide protection; to bring hidden truths to light

Kunzite—to dissolve emotional blockages; to facilitate honest introspection

Peridot—to release resentment and tap in to joy; to enhance confidence and self-worth

Lepidolite—to support emotional healing and stress relief; to enhance relaxation and sleep

Pink calcite—to foster self-love and compassion, to support emotional healing and forgiveness

Malachite—to flush out negative energy; to promote personal transformation

Pink chalcedony—to foster love and compassion; to promote emotional healing and inner peace

Moonstone—to enhance intuition and promote emotional balance; to spark new beginnings

Pink tourmaline—to prioritize self-care; to set healthy boundaries

Morganite—to heal old emotional wounds; to gently nurture the heart

Red jasper—to provide stability and grounding; to enhance vitality and strength

Rhodochrosite—to promote a positive outlook on love; to boost self-esteem

 Selenite—to cleanse and purify energy; to promote clarity and spiritual connection

 Rhodonite—to foster emotional healing and balance; to stimulate forgiveness

 Smoky quartz—to release negative energy and promote grounding; to support stress relief

 Rose quartz—to promote love and compassion; to enhance beauty and pleasure

 Tiger's eye—to promote courage and personal power; to support manifestation and decision-making

 Ruby—to enhance passion and vitality; to release limiting beliefs

 Unakite—to support healing, spiritual growth, and self-discovery; to instill patience

CONCLUSION

As our time together comes to a close, I want to remind you, dear reader, of a powerful truth: self-love is a continuous practice. It's not a one-time event or a quick fix. Moving forward on this path means committing to yourself again and again. Granted, there will be days when loving yourself feels like a Herculean task, but guess what? That's totally okay. We all have those days, and it doesn't make you any less deserving of love and kindness. In fact, it's precisely in these tough moments that self-compassion becomes crucial.

Whenever you encounter self-doubt or setbacks, remember to be gentle with yourself. After all, self-love isn't about perfection; it's about owning who you are, flaws and all. Embrace your vulnerabilities, for they are stepping stones to deeper self-acceptance and a gateway to your one-of-a-kind magick.

Last but not least, I want to thank each and every one of you from the bottom of my heart. Words can't begin to express how grateful I am for your support. While it's been an honor and a privilege to share these lessons with you, know that your story doesn't end here. Crystals are just one tool on your self-love journey, and this book is only the beginning. Continue to explore and expand beyond these pages, and find what sets your heart ablaze.

With heartfelt gratitude and love,

Katie

FURTHER READING

Crystal Zodiac: An Astrological Guide to Enhancing Your Life with Crystals by Katie Huang (2020, Houghton Mifflin)

For anyone new to the benefits of crystal healing and astrology, or for those who have been practicing for years, *Crystal Zodiac* breaks down their practical, easy-to-use applications, showing how they powerfully work together to prioritize personal growth and mindfulness in the day-to-day.

Luminous Dreams: Explore the Abundant Magic and Hidden Meanings in Your Dreams by Katie Huang (2022, Chronicle)

This beautifully illustrated, soothing guide invites readers to explore the world of dreams through a collection of bedtime rituals, dream symbols, and intuitive practices.

Crystal Moods by Katie Huang (2023, The Book Shop Ltd)

Explore the connection between crystals and emotions with this interactive kit that includes seven foundational stones, a 120-page book, and full color chakra poster.

ALSO AVAILABLE IN THIS SERIES:

Self-Love Potions by Cosmic Valeria (2023, Leaping Hare Press)

ABOUT THE AUTHOR

Katie Huang is the founder of Love By Luna, a leading astrological lifestyle brand. With her extensive knowledge of astrology and crystal healing, she has penned two transformative books, *Crystal Zodiac: An Astrological Guide to Enhancing Your Life with Crystals*, and, *Luminous Dreams: Explore the Abundant Magic and Hidden Meanings in Your Dreams*. Her insightful work has been featured in numerous publications such as Forbes, Cosmopolitan, Teen Vogue, and Marie Claire. As a wellness entrepreneur and mental health advocate, Katie is passionate about developing accessible tools for mindful living, and strives to empower individuals in their personal and spiritual growth. She resides in Santa Monica, California.

ABOUT THE ILLUSTRATOR

Marie-Noël Dumont is an illustrator and graphic designer. She finds creative inspiration for her whimsical and botanical drawings in the beautiful nature of southern Quebec, where she lives with her partner and her two kids. Find out more about her work at dumontdesigngraphique.com.

INDEX

First published in 2024 by Leaping Hare Press
an imprint of The Quarto Group.
One Triptych Place, London, SE1 9SH
United Kingdom
T (0)20 7700 6700
www.Quarto.com

A catalogue record for this book is available
from the British Library.

ISBN 978-0-7112-9079-2
Ebook 978-0-7112-9080-8

Printed in China
10 9 8 7 6 5 4 3 2 1

Illustrations by Marie-Noël Dumont
Design by Nikki Ellis
Senior Commissioning Editor: Monica Perdoni
Project Manager: Chloe Murphy
Assistant Editor: Katerina Menhennet
Senior Designer: Renata Latipova
Production Controller: Maeve Healey and
    Rohana Yusof

Chakra symbols on pages 17-20 adapted
from Ramziya Khusnullina, accessed via
Shutterstock.